THE
MANTRAP
GARDEN

THE MANTRAP GARDEN

JOHN SHERWOOD

CHARLES SCRIBNER'S SONS
NEW YORK

This novel is a work of fiction. Names, characters, places and incidents are either the product of the author's imagination or are used fictitiously. Any resemblance to actual persons, living or dead, events or locales is entirely coincidental.

Library of Congress Cataloging-in-Publication Data

Sherwood, John, 1913-
   The mantrap garden.

   I. Title.
PR6037.H517M3   1986   823'.914   86-11818
ISBN 0-684-18726-4

First American Edition

Printed in the United States of America.

NOTE

Gertrude Jekyll lived from 1843 to 1932, and took up gardening in 1891 when weak eyesight made it impossible for her to continue as an artist. Her writings on horticulture, from which the quotations in the footnotes are taken, had a decisive influence on the development of the modern garden. The most notable in her long list of publications are *Wood and Garden* (1899) *Wall and Water Gardens* (1901) and, most important, *Colour in the Flower Garden* (1908).

ONE

"OH DEAR, I had been counting on you," said Graham Harrison, addressing himself to the pink blob in the middle of his field of vision. "You can't let me down."

"I'm sorry," said the pink blob. "I really must say 'no'."

"But I'm eighty," Harrison protested. "My doctor says it's time I gave up crises. It's someone else's turn."

"Not mine," said the pink blob firmly. "What you need is a bossy administrative lady with a social conscience."

One corner of his left eye still functioned after a fashion. He directed it at the pink blob, which resolved itself into a sleeveless summer dress. This was surrounded by a huge brown blur. After wondering why some optical quirk of senility had made the leather armchair seem very large, he remembered that the woman sitting in it was very small.

"I really am much too busy," said an indistinct area at the head end of the summer dress.

"But unless something is done now we'll have a tragedy on our hands. Do please consider it seriously, Mrs Grant. The trustees meet once a month at most. You can't call that an excessive demand on your time."

"It sounds simple," said Celia Grant, "but I know these voluntary things. They suck you into a vortex, before you know where you are you're down the plug hole working your fingers to the bone."

Harrison wished he could see her better. From what he vaguely remembered or could discern with his erratic left eye, she was in her forties, though the contents of the summer dress were shapely and young looking. He also detected silver-grey hair, which must surely be premature, surmounting pretty,

7

rather doll-like features which gave an impression of helplessness. But a woman who had made a resounding success, in a very short time, of a specialist nursery garden could hardly be as urgently in need of care and protection as her fragile appearance suggested.

"I wish I could help," she said. "But the business is expanding far too fast for comfort, the mail orders are coming in already. How I shall get through the autumn I can't imagine."

"Those mail orders," he murmured, with sixty years' experience of the horticultural industry behind him. "A nightmare, even when they fill in the order forms correctly. Oh dear, the trustees will be very disappointed, Mrs Grant. They know of your standing in the horticultural world, and they welcomed the idea whole-heartedly."

"What exactly is wrong at Monk's Mead?" Celia asked, to change the subject a little.

"Everything! Bare patches in the Long Borders! They ought to be looking their best now, but it breaks my heart to see them. The Blue Garden's infested with bindweed, and the Michaelmas daisies in the October Garden haven't been staked with brushwood, they're growing up through hideous plastic arrangements supported on bright yellow canes. The polyanthus primroses this spring were a disgrace. They weren't divided last year and what they're calling the Munstead Strain would make poor Miss Jekyll turn in her grave. A famous garden that's open to the public can't afford to look scruffy, and the word's getting round. Attendances have been falling off, they're less than half Sissinghurst's now, and they need the entrance money to keep going."

"Isn't there an endowment under the trust?"

"Of course, but it's the usual story, alas. Inflation has reduced the endowment to a barely perceptible drop in the bottom of the bucket."

"I went round Monk's Mead once when my husband was alive," said Celia. "It was looking rather good then."

"Ah, that was before the old lady got bedridden. She was a slave-driver, nothing escaped her eye."

"So the garden started to go downhill when she took to her bed?"

"Gradually, yes. But the deterioration only became really shocking after she died in January."

"If things are as bad as you say," Celia objected, "someone's got to do a full-time trouble shooting job. There's no point in me going to a meeting once a month and scolding like a shrew."

"On the contrary, that's just what's needed. Let me explain. When the trust was set up, nearly forty years ago, the board consisted of Mrs Mortlock herself, and five trustees from outside, people of real standing in the horticultural world. But as the members of the original board died or resigned, they were replaced by members of the family. That was quite wrong, because they're all involved in the day-to-day running of the garden. They can't take a detached view and their interests aren't necessarily those of the trust. While old Mrs Mortlock had everything under her eye that didn't matter, she ran the show impeccably. Now she's gone, and the younger generation have got slack. I'm the only outside trustee left to act as a watchdog and keep them up to the mark, and I'm past it."

He turned and treated Celia to a rueful grin. "You've put me in an awkward situation, Mrs Grant. I had every intention of dying as soon as a favourable opportunity presents itself, but I can't do that till I've left the responsibility for Monk's Mead in good hands."

"I'm sorry," said Celia.

"Will you do me one favour before you finally decide? Go there and have a look round. When you see one of the world's historic gardens going to rack and ruin, you might just take pity on it and change your mind."

Celia thought about this. She had intended to devote the rest of the afternoon to the promising-looking progeny of two dwarf hypericums that she had crossed. The seedlings urgently needed pricking out. But old people who got ideas into their heads ought to be humoured and Monk's Mead was only a mile or two off her route home. A quick look round would probably confirm her hunch that the allegations of rack and ruin were

9

exaggerated; a tetchy carry-on triggered off by defective eyesight and pernickety old age.

"Very well, I'll look in there," she promised.

"Oh, thank you. I'm sure you'll change your mind, and then I can stop being wonderful for my age."

The car park at Monk's Mead was huge, probably larger than the garden, and almost full. The long line of tourist coaches included some from abroad, and Celia suspected that Harrison was wrong about falling attendances. Before getting out of the car she fished up a crumpled head-scarf and sun-glasses out of the sordid muddle in the glove locker and put them on by way of disguise, for she had no intention of getting entangled with the Mortlock family during her undercover tour of inspection. She had met the old lady's daughter and son-in-law once at a grand dinner party. To be caught spying out the land and deciding not to be a trustee would be embarrassing.

The car park must once have been a field. There was an admirable old barn in one corner, weatherboarded and roofed in mellow tiles, which proved on a closer view to provide teas and light refreshments. Beside the barn was the entrance gate to the garden, flanked by a large notice:

MONK'S MEAD
THE HISTORIC GARDEN CREATED BY GERTRUDE JEKYLL

Details followed of opening times and admission charges, which were steep. She paid, and bought a guide book for good measure.

Glancing at it before proceeding further, she discovered a lengthy introduction:

The garden at Monk's Mead was created in the early years of this century under the supervision of Gertrude Jekyll, whose pioneering work and example formed a dominating influence on the development of the modern garden. . . .

Fair enough, Celia thought. The way the English gardened had been altered for all time by the formidable old spinster's anathema on carpet bedding and her propaganda for the herbaceous border. Celia and her husband had visited Jekyll-influenced gardens as far afield as San Francisco and Hong Kong. However, to continue:

> Miss Jekyll devoted almost as much attention to the garden of her friend Cedric Mortlock at Monk's Mead as she did to her own ten miles away at Munstead Wood. It is one of the few surviving examples of her gardening style to have survived intact since its creation. Great care has been taken to conform to her original planting schemes, and no plants introduced after her time have been used in the garden.

This sort of talk always made Celia uneasy. A garden was a living organism, not a museum. It could not be made to stop growing and stand still unless it was a grand Frenchified affair consisting of statues and fountains and things one could clip like yew and box. Besides, go-getting old Gertrude would have been the last person to put a garden in mothballs and ignore all the valuable garden subjects that had come into cultivation since her day. Celia shuddered, convinced that Monk's Mead would give her the creeps, and dived into the guide book again. But indigestible family history followed concerning successive generations of Mortlocks who had somehow nursed the garden through two world wars and sundry other crises, till in 1948 the widow of the last male Mortlock had set up a trust to "preserve for all time a monument to a decisive turning point in gardening history".

Enough of this, thought Celia, and went through the wicket gate into the garden. Steered by the plan in her guide book, she made her way through the Wild Garden, in which there was nothing much to see. It was August, and the bulbs and azaleas and rhododendrons planted in clearings among oak and silver birch trees were long out of flower. But presently the house came into view on the far side of the lawn, a subtle blend of cottagey gables and dormers by Miss Jekyll's architect friend Edwin Lutyens. Catching sight of it gave Celia another uneasy pang. The garden was designed to be explored outwards from the house. She was seeing it back to front.

The lawn was full of noisy people, as was to be expected at an August weekend. Skirting round the thickest part of the crowd, she crossed it to an archway near the house, for the way to the Long Borders lay through the Lily Court, a typical Jekyll feature with hydrangeas and maiden's wreath and hostas in tubs round a waterlily pool with steps leading down into the water. The court was enclosed at one end by the house. At the other, beyond the pool, stood a nude statue of a youth with an inscription on the plinth:

ANTHONY MORTLOCK
Poet and Soldier
1918–1942
Beyond the wall of smoke lies death's harsh garden.
If I should fall there shed no tears for me,
But rather, seek our generation's pardon,
Plant finer gardens for posterity.

Celia had been vaguely aware of a second world war poet called Anthony Mortlock, but had forgotten his connection with Monk's Mead. There was a stone seat* against the wall of the house, and she sat down to find out more from the guide book. Anthony, she discovered, was the Mortlocks' son, and the sculpture had been done from life when he was seventeen. There followed a lyrical description of the intelligence, charm, and love of the Monk's Mead garden which had marked his tragically short life. After spending the first part of the second world war in a safe intelligence job, he had insisted on leaving it in 1941 and joining a combat unit. He had been killed in action a year later.

For Mrs Mortlock, a widow, losing an only son must have been a mortal blow, but she had expressed her anguish

---

*"Though stone seats uncushioned are barely admissible in our climate, yet it may be remembered that in passing from the garden to the house, in nine times out of ten it will be the eye only that will repose upon them. And in hottest summer, when they will actually be in use, it is easy to provide such cushions for the seat and back, and some beautiful mat of oriental weave of quiet colouring for the feet, as may ensure complete and wholesome comfort." (G.J.)

embarrassingly. One could see at a glance that the sculpture commemorating him was not an idealized youth-symbol but a portrait of handsome young Anthony Mortlock with no clothes on. Was it quite fitting for a dead soldier to be stuck up on a plinth and exposed, genitals and all, to the gaze of the chattering parents and sweet-eating children who were passing by all the time? And would these paying customers grasp that his plea to "plant finer gardens" did not refer literally to richer composts and improved varieties of dahlia?

These thoughts were interrupted by sounds of domestic battle in the house behind her. She turned, for her seat backed on to a window, but there was a net curtain over it which frustrated curiosity. A stormy argument was going on between a man and a woman. The words were too muffled to hear but the tones of voice were enough. The woman was in great distress, sobbing and crying out in great gusts of protest. The man was being maddeningly logical in a loud, boring voice, and one could tell from her reaction that logic was irrelevant, he had missed the point. Celia's sympathies were all with her, especially when he refused to listen and began to bellow, but she rose abruptly and moved away. She wanted nothing to do with this garden and its inmates, even as an eavesdropper.

An archway led from the Lily Court into a paved walk under a pergola, which must have been quite a sight in early summer when the wisteria covering it was in flower. According to the plan in the guide book, a maze of enclosures opened off it containing a White Garden, Silver and Gold Gardens, and umpteen other theme gardens devoted to particular seasons or colours. But Celia struck out through another archway into the walled garden containing the Long Borders, to see if they were really in as bad a state as Graham Harrison claimed. This was the main summer attraction that everyone had come to see, a double border two hundred feet long and fourteen feet wide on either side of a broad gravel path. It was described at length in all the Jekyll literature, and Celia remembered it vividly from her visit with Roger ten years ago as perfect, unlike any modern border, and in some indefinable way slightly "sick". Its colour scheme started at the ends with pastel shades and worked up through stronger and deeper colours towards the climax in the middle, a riot of orange and crimson and scarlet. As with all Jekyll designs the foliage, much of it grey or grey-blue, was as carefully considered as the flowers.

Keeping all this looking its best for three months must be slavery. According to the books, when anything went out of flower one had to pull forward something else, a clematis or a group of *Helianthus salicifolius** growing behind it, to cover the ugly remains. One must also wheel in barrowloads of what Miss Jekyll called "drop-in plants", pot plants brought on into flower elsewhere, which one plunged complete with pot into the remaining gaps. All this on top of the routine work of keeping two enormous borders tidy.

Seen from one end the display looked presentable. But as Celia advanced down the central path she saw that Harrison was right, all was far from well. Plants that had gone out of flower had not been replaced by "drop-ins" or the gaps had been filled with unsuitable plant material that clashed with the colour scheme. Whatever was a hideous red and white pelargonium called "Aztec" (but privately christened "Montezuma's Revenge" by Celia) doing in a border designed years before it was misbegotten by its breeder? Moreover someone had "dropped in" hydrangeas without observing Miss Jekyll's decree that their leaves, which were an objectionably bright green, had to be hidden behind something else.

Half way down the border a man in overalls, obviously a gardener, was standing watching the crowd. He had iron-grey hair and a cleft chin, and Celia had seen him somewhere before. Where, though? Puzzled, she strolled on till her eye was caught by a group of deep purple phloxes with a white eye, with blue campanulas planted behind them. Worse and worse, she thought, Miss Jekyll never mixed blue with purple. And the phloxes were too vivid and modern-looking, they could almost have come from her own nursery. . . .

*Miss Jekyll wrote of it as *H. orygalis*, but since then the name-changing botanical pundits have been at work.

14

They had, she realized with a start. She knew now where she had seen the gardener with the cleft chin before. A month ago, was it? Perhaps six weeks. She had thought it odd at the time. He had arrived at the nursery with a pick-up. Not content with buying all the phloxes and *Aster frikartii* she would let him have, he had cleared out her stock of various other things that were coming into flower and could be used to fill gaps in a summer border. It was obvious what had happened at Monk's Mead. The reserve of drop-in plants had run out unexpectedly (Why? There must have been serious mismanagement) and garden centres for miles around had been ransacked for anything available to keep the borders furnished.

And here was another puzzle: a second gardener, a youngish man, standing stock still in the middle of the path and staring at the crowd in the same way as his cleft-chin colleague further back along the border. They were sentries, she realized, making no bones about the fact that they were on the watch and ready to pounce on anyone doing wilful damage. Moreover they were not the only sentries.

A dark hawk-faced man in his forties had been hovering in the Lily Court while she was sitting there, she had wondered why. Perhaps there were others, it was extraordinary. Most gardens open to the public took unobtrusive precautions against pilfering, but this was in a different league.

Pondering these mysteries, she decided to cross-check on Harrison's other grumble: were the famous Munstead Strain primroses* also in a parlous state? That meant doubling back into the Wild Garden. It could be reached through a door in the wall half way down the Long Borders, which opened on to a maze of grass paths winding through plantings of holly and silver birch. She would never have found the primroses without the map in the guide book, but saw at once that Harrison was right. Most of the clumps were huge and too starved-looking to flower properly and there were dry seed-heads everywhere.

---

*Miss Jekyll developed the Munstead Strain of primroses by crossing the variety Golden Plover with a very pale, almost white polyanthus found in a cottage garden. The flowers are all white and yellow, but vary greatly in detail.

They should have been lifted and divided as soon as the display was finished, but the beds had not been dug over. They were infested with ground elder and dog mercury. Next year's display would be a disaster.

Wondering why this had been allowed to happen, she walked on till she came to a clearing where an even more shocking sight brought her up standing: the wreckage of a specimen tree that had been — there was no other word for it — murdered. Its trunk had been hacked through brutally, five feet from the ground, leaving a few miserable side branches which Celia examined with increasing horror. There was no mistaking those enormously long leaves, glaucous underneath, and the huge seed-case. This had once been a superb specimen of *Magnolia macrophylla*, a magnificent species with larger leaves and flowers than any other deciduous tree hardy in the British Isles. Cunning old Gertrude had sited it against a background of dark evergreens to form one of her "garden pictures" as she called them. Underplanted with kalmias and ferns it must have been a superb sight, and someone had cut it down.

Why? Disease? The leaves on the remaining branches looked perfectly healthy, and the snaggy cut was not the work of a skilled tree surgeon. More and more puzzled, she walked on. Presently a side path marked "Private" led off into a thicket, probably hiding a working area with compost heaps and tool sheds. Had the top of the magnolia been hidden away in there? In any case, this was a temptation not to be resisted. One could tell a lot about how well a garden was run by looking at the parts visitors were not meant to see.

There was no one about, so she stole in. But the thicket hid no working area, only a large rubbish pit of the sort often made in unfrequented parts of a wild garden to rot down weeds and soft prunings. However it contained no ordinary rubbish. A huge planting of helianthus had been cut down in full flower, only a few hours ago by the look of it. Why? And what was wrong with the foliage, it had turned a sickly yellow and some of the leaves looked deformed. The same fate seemed to have overtaken

16

clumps of coreopsis and bergamot and what must once have been some pale pink dahlias. No disease looked like that. An accident with a sprayer? If so, it was on a tremendous scale. The rubbish pit was half full.

The remains of the magnolia were nowhere to be seen, perhaps they had been burnt. Celia's mind jerked back to the other puzzle, the ostentatious policing of the Long Borders and the ominous gaps in them. The conclusion was clear. The garden was being systematically vandalized. A specimen tree had been wrecked, clumps of plants had been deliberately drenched with weedkiller while they were in full flower. Before the damage became too obvious, they had been cut down and hurried away out of sight in this pit.

It had been dug very recently. Unexpectedly the path went on past it and out on the far side of the thicket, and there was another "Private" notice warning off intruders coming in the opposite direction. Everything, the freshly dug pit, its siting beside an existing path, the pair of notices, spoke of hasty improvisation to meet an emergency.

"Can I help you?" said a man's voice sharply. "You seem to have lost your way."

It was the man who had been mounting guard in the Lily Court, he must have run across to her when he saw her vanish into the forbidden thicket, for he was leaning against a tree and pretending not to be out of breath. Fortyish, perhaps, dark and sharp-featured like a hawk eyeing a mouse. Jeans and a bush shirt. He was staring at her hard, as if trying to see behind the disguising sun-glasses.

"I'm afraid I was trespassing," she said. "I saw a willow warbler go in here and I followed it."

He grinned savagely. "Are you sure it was a willow warbler? What colour were its legs?"

What indeed, thought Celia, and wished she had told a lie which did not require her to distinguish between anonymous-looking little brown birds. "Paleish," she ventured after careful thought.

"Then it was probably a chiffchaff."

17

This was so obviously a test that she said: "I thought a chiffchaff's legs were dark."

He grinned again and said "well done" with a mocking intonation which meant "well guessed". But the grin was a nervous reflex, for some reason he was more frightened of her than she was of him.

"You ought to see the Long Borders," he suggested jerkily. "They're looking marvellous, it's this way, I'll show you."

Feeling as if she had been caught shoplifting, she let him shepherd her along the winding path through the wood. Why was she being hustled away? Was the vandalizing of the garden supposed to be a secret? She would have to think about that later, he was obviously a member of the family and he was interrogating her.

"Working for a newspaper must be quite interesting," he said.

"Bad for the digestion, I'm told. D'you know any journalists?"

"No, aren't you one?"

"Goodness no, what made you think that?"

"The ruthless curiosity with which you pursued the alleged willow warbler. What brought you into the Wild Garden anyway, there's nothing worth seeing in there in August."

"Miss Jekyll would squash you like a greenfly for saying that. She thought leaves and stems were just as well worth looking at as flowers."

"How intriguing, you've actually read her. Do tell me who you are, d'you live near here?"

"No, about fifteen miles away," said Celia as the house came into view at the end of a glade. "Goodness, what a cunning old lady she was, look how beautifully she's managed the transition* from woodland to lawns and flowerbeds. . . ."

---

*"When woodland adjoins garden ground there is too often a sudden jolt; the wood ends in a hard line, sometimes with a path along it. It would have been better if the garden had not been brought so close to the wood. In such a case the path would go, not next the trees but along the middle of neutral ground, and would be so planted as to belong equally to garden and wood." (G.J.)

She managed to keep up this line of talk till they were back on the lawn among the sightseers, where there was hope of shaking him off. But as they started out across the grass a tall agitated-looking woman in her sixties with wild grey hair came cantering out of the crowd and bore down on Celia like a simple-minded tragedy queen. She wore a social smile like a comic mask over her agitation, and it took Celia a moment or two to realize that this was the Mortlock daughter, whom she had met at the dinner party. The Mortlock daughter had evidently recognized her despite her disguise, which was awkward. She had been caught spying and now she would have to say, "Good afternoon, I've been asked to be a trustee, but on looking round your garden I've decided that the answer is a very firm 'no'."

But there was no crisis after all. The person being approached and smiled at was not herself but her hawk-faced escort.

"Adam darling, where on *earth* have you been, we've been searching the undergrowth for you."

Adam must be the son, there had been talk of a son at the dinner party. What was the Mortlock daughter's married name? Lindsay, that was it. Lady Lindsay, because her husband had just retired with honour from the upper reaches of the Civil Service. But what had happened to her? She was haggard and unrecognizable; at the dinner party she had been enormous fun. The uncontrolled grey hair and clumsy movements did not matter, she was so obviously happy and popular, perhaps surprised as well as pleased to find herself so. She must have been a tall, gawky girl; one could imagine her gradually overcoming an agonizing shyness and building up enough self-confidence to enjoy her life and make a success of it. But that sort of confidence is fragile and hers had been shattered, one had only to look at her ravaged face. Her eyes were red with weeping, she was undoubtedly the female partner in the noisy domestic scene that Celia had overheard from her seat against the wall of the house.

"Adam! Mary! What in heaven's name are you doing here?" The hectoring voice belonged unmistakably to the male partner in the same scene. Adam put an arm round his mother. It was clear which side he was on in the family line-up.

Sir Julian Lindsay, who now stood glaring in cold anger at his wild-haired wife, was a complete contrast to her, a neatly dressed six-footer with beautifully arranged white hair, so distinguished-looking that it amounted to caricature. He was a presence rather than a person, and could have been mistaken for a photographic model projecting integrity and sound judgment in an advertisement for an investment trust.

Mary Lindsay looked guilty. Adam got between them and embarked on a fresh explanation which Sir Julian cut short with a gesture. He had caught them idling on the lawn when they should have been on sentry-go against vandals in more vulnerable parts of the garden, and he led them off in disgrace towards the Lily Court to take up their posts.

Not wishing to encounter them again and have to explain herself, Celia started off towards the car park, but stopped after a few yards. Someone was screaming hysterically in the Lily Court. People ran across the lawn towards it. Celia ran too. Sightseers had poured into it through all the entrances. Julian Lindsay had his wife in his arms and was shouting "Stop it Mary, pull yourself together", but it was not a loving husband's embrace. He was behind her, pinning her arms to her sides, trying to drag her away and end an embarrassing public scene.

But Mary stood transfixed, staring across the pool with its lilies at her brother's statue. A rope slung over the wall behind it ended in a noose round its neck. It had been dressed in an outrageously padded bra and a long skirt, a get-up which made the expression on the sensitively chiselled features suddenly look obscene. People in the crowd of gapers began to snigger, but stopped when they saw what lay at Anthony Mortlock's feet; something protruding from an infant's white woolly shawl, with a severed bloody neck and no head.

"That was awful, Julian, A real Hammer Films shocker."

"I daresay, but another time, Mary, try to take a grip on yourself. Remember, keeping calm is half the battle."

"I'm sorry, I did try. But this was the worst yet, what was it in the shawl?"

"A piglet."

"It stank. They kept it till it stank, then put it there. And fancy doing that to Anthony's statue. They know how fond I was of him, how upset I'd be."

"Nonsense, a nude statue is an obvious target for these people. It was Adam's fault, what was he doing rushing off like that into the Wild Garden? He's supposed to watch the Lily Court as well as that end of the Long Borders."

"He saw that woman snooping around the thicket where the rubbish pit is, the one in the head-scarf and dark glasses. He was afraid she was a journalist so he went after her."

"Did he ask her who she was?"

"Of course, but she wouldn't say. That was meant to be me, wasn't it? They dressed up Anthony's statue like that to say I was a murderess. I shall asphyxiate with shame if this gets into the Press."

"If it does, it does. There's nothing we can do."

"If she wasn't a journalist, what was she? A television personality drawing attention to herself by parading about in disguise? Julian, I can't stand much more of this, when will it stop?"

"Why d'you keep asking me that, how do I know? All we can do is, pretend it's not happening and hope for the best."

Celia spent Sunday pottering round the glasshouses at Archer-scroft Nurseries, repainting the front door of her cottage, and trying to convince herself that the trials and tribulations of the Monk's Mead garden were none of her business. She was deeply sorry for Mary Lindsay, and could not stop wondering what had reduced her to such a shattered state. But life had taught her, among other things, that trying to organize other people's lives for them was a waste of time.

Late that night Bill Wilkins dropped in for a chat with his employer on his way home from a weekend in London with his girl friend. No one would have guessed from his weekend attire that he was the hard-working head gardener of a fast-growing nursery business. The designer jeans, Italian hand-made shoes and expensive haircut represented the taste of the girl friend, a masterful young executive with a high-powered property agency. Celia disapproved of her and had made discreet attempts to break it up, but in vain. He was fanatically faithful to her and let her bully him mercilessly. Celia suspected her of flaunting him as a status symbol, for he was a ridiculously handsome young man with dramatic blue eyes and hair so blond that he looked slightly unreal, like Marilyn Monroe. She opened a window surreptitiously. As usual, he had come back from London smelling powerfully of the most expensive male toiletries money could buy.

"You told them 'no' about Monk's Mead?" he asked.

"I'm still thinking about it."

"Oh Celia, be careful. Trustees have to go to meetings and sign things and rap the people's fingers if they've been at the cash box. We're rushed off our feet, it's frantic, we haven't the time."

"There might be advantages for the business," Celia argued, not very honestly. "I had a look round there yesterday and, d'you know, they don't have a plant stall. They can't grow plants for sale because there's nowhere to do it without wrecking the Gertrude Jekyll layout, which is sacrosanct. That gave me an idea."

Bill fixed her with wide blue eyes and nodded solemnly. "Oh I get it Celia. We grow the plants and take a stall there. And the people come out of the garden all starry-eyed and they see the stall and they say 'ooh lovely, we saw those inside, let's have one'."

"Exactly, it's an ideal point of sale for us. We increase our turnover without increasing the mail orders and having to hire yet more of those idiotic girls for the packing shed."

To her fury he was shaking with laughter, the solemn nods had been an act. "Come off it, Celia, how could we ever grow enough? We've an order book as long as the Sydney Harbour Bridge already. I know you, you don't fool me. You're on the prowl."

"Nonsense, what d'you mean, prowl?"

"When you see a mystery you go mad with curiosity and start to itch, then you prowl."

"Well, why shouldn't I? You rush off to London and drench yourself in expensive scent, why shouldn't I have a hobby too?"

He grinned. "Okay then, so there's a mystery at Monk's Mead. Tell us all about it."

"The garden's being vandalized. There's a woman there who's frightened and desperately unhappy and I don't understand what's going on."

He made her describe her observations at Monk's Mead, then said: "Well, there's no need for you to go on the prowl there because I can solve your mystery for you now. There's tricks being played in that garden on account of that dodgy inquest back in the winter. You remember, it was all in the paper."

"I never read the sordid bits of the paper."

"Oh Celia you liar, of course you do. Wait though, you was still in New Zealand, on the prowl after the mad Lord that grew Alpines, that's why you missed it. The inquest was on the old lady there at Monk's Mead, what was her name?"

"Mrs Mortlock."

"That's right, she was ninety and her arthritis hurt her a lot and she said she didn't want to live. And there she was stuffed full of sleeping pills, and the doctor and everyone tried to cover up. But you could see it was a mercy killing by the daughter, it stood out a mile. There was a lot of bad feeling about it locally, people saying she shouldn't have, mercy killing's wrong. And now someone's punishing her. The noose and the king-size bra and so on was pointing the finger at her for murder."

"If she's supposed to have murdered her elderly mother, where does the beheaded piglet-baby fit in, it's the wrong age-group."

"Maybe she killed a baby too."

"What baby? Anyway, you haven't solved my mystery."

"Most of it."

"No. You've told me why. I want to know who."

TWO

"MERCY KILLING DENIED," Celia read in a large front-page headline. The local paper, produced from the archives of the Guildford public library by a helpful assistant, gave a very full account of the inquest on Mrs Mortlock. It overflowed from the front page and continued amid the advertisements for second-hand cars and washing machines inside.

. . . Lady Lindsay then gave evidence. She stated that on the day of Mrs Mortlock's death she had arranged to drive her cleaning woman to hospital for a specialist's appointment. A neighbour, Mrs Hall, was to have covered her absence from the house and given Mrs Mortlock her tea, but it later appeared that Mrs Hall thought the hospital appointment was for the following day.

Asked by the coroner how the misunderstanding had arisen, Lady Lindsay could give no explanation. Continuing, she said that when it was time to leave for the hospital Mrs Hall had not arrived. As there was no reply from her house Lady Lindsay assumed that she was on her way and left, rather than let her cleaning woman miss an appointment with a busy specialist and be put at the end of his waiting list.

An X-ray was found to be necessary, so she was at the hospital far longer than she expected. When she returned home her husband was already back from his office in London and told her that her mother had been rushed to hospital in a coma, but had died in the ambulance.

The Coroner: "The evidence suggests that she had taken at least twenty of her sleeping tablets. Were they kept within her reach?"

Lady Lindsay: "No, that's what's so dreadful, I can't understand it. She talked of wanting to die and it worried me, so I always kept them in the bathroom, out of her way."

The Coroner: "But she was taking them regularly?"

Lady Lindsay: "Yes, two every night. She had trouble sleeping because of the pain."

The Coroner: "Could she have concealed and accumulated enough to make up an overdose?"

Lady Lindsay: "I don't see how. I gave her them with water and she swallowed them."

The Coroner: "Lady Lindsay, did you consider her death a merciful release?"

Lady Lindsay: "Of course. One must be sensible. She knew her life was over, she was hoping to die."

The Coroner: "I have to put this to you. Did you place enough tablets to make a lethal dose within Mrs Mortlock's reach for her to take if she wished, and arrange for her to be left unattended till it was too late for her to be found?"

Lady Lindsay: "Oh how horrible. She was my mother, I could never have brought myself to do such a thing. How could you make such a dreadful suggestion?"

At this point Lady Lindsay became distressed and was allowed to leave the courtroom.

Celia could imagine the unfortunate impression that the tall, awkward woman with her larger-than-life gestures would make as a witness. She looked and behaved like an eccentric, and eccentrics were seldom given the benefit of the doubt. Everyone else including the coroner had bent over backwards to let her down lightly. The doctor had been splendidly vague about how many tablets ought to have been left over in the bottle in the bathroom. He, the vicar and the district nurse had been lavish in their praise of Mary Lindsay's devoted nursing of her mother, as also had a Miss Barbara Seymour, described as "the eminent educationalist" and a close friend of the family.

Miss Seymour gave evidence that she visited Mrs Mortlock regularly. She had last seen her a week before her death and found her perfectly lucid despite pain-killing drugs, and very grateful to her daughter for her devoted care. Asked if she thought Mrs Mortlock capable of planning and executing her own demise, Miss Seymour replied: "Certainly, given the means. On two occasions she asked me to provide them but of course I refused."

Sir Julian said what was proper in support of his wife, and took the blame for the confusion over the date when the cleaning woman had to be taken to hospital. A discordant note was then struck by Mrs Hall, the neighbour who had failed to appear and look after Mrs Mortlock. Exuding venom from every pore, she said it was not her fault if she had not come on the day she was expected, she had made a note in her diary at the time, the Lindsays had misled her. According to her the old lady, whom she had often looked after while the family was out, was mentally confused, full of complaints of maltreatment by her family, and so helpless that she could hardly help herself to a drink of water, let alone poison herself. Mrs Hall added before she could be stopped that she was a God-fearing woman and it was no use calling it nice things like euthanasia or mercy killing. Lady Lindsay was guilty of mortal sin and should go to prison for it.

This tasteless outburst did not, however, swing the verdict against Mary. She had left the house unlocked so that Mrs Hall, who had no key, could get in. The Coroner pointed out that anyone could have walked in and provided the fatal dose; there was no means of knowing how the tablets had got into Mrs Mortlock's possession. An open verdict should therefore be returned.

Celia began making a list of the questions not answered by the newspaper report. Was Sir Julian lying to protect his wife when he took the blame for making the wrong date with Mrs Hall? Had she been asked which of them spoke to her about it, and if so how had she answered? What was Barbara Seymour's connection with the family?

"Barbara? Must we, Julian? She and Mother didn't get on, Mother
26

always said she'd never have her on the board."

"Your mother bullied you all her life, my dear Mary. I shall not let her order you about from beyond the grave."

"But Barbara's a horticultural hooligan. That jobbing gardener of hers plants calceolarias, and she lets him."

"As a busy professional woman she has to delegate the domesticities. She'd be an asset on the board, she has a first class administrative mind."

"I don't like her, you know that."

"Yes, but as usual your thought-processes are a mystery to me."

"She's like some loathsome pedigree cat, putting on airs and despising me as a brainless goose. Graham Harrison's dead against having her too."

"No, Mary. Harrison's point was, we ought to replace him with someone from outside with good horticultural experience. He won't be satisfied till we've done that, but we have two vacancies to fill, his and your mother's. We can vote the Grant woman into one and Barbara into the other."

"I hate the idea of the Grant woman even more than Barbara. We've always decided things for ourselves, why must we have a total stranger pushing her nasty nose in?"

"Because Harrison insists on us having an outside point of view on the board, he won't budge on that. If we don't settle for Mrs Grant we may get someone far more inquisitive and difficult."

"How d'you know she isn't both?"

"We met her that night at the Farninghams, surely you remember? A tiny little woman, rather helpless-looking, with white hair. We talked gardens most of the time, I don't think she knows or cares about anything else. She'll be far too busy with that nursery of hers to hang around here asking inconvenient questions."

Celia drove towards Monk's Mead with her mind still not made up. Julian's invitation had been charmingly put. "*Do* come. About half-past ten? Perfect, then we can have a chat and a look round the garden before the public arrive in their hordes. Without obligation, of course. Then you'll know what you'll be letting yourself in for if you decide to come to our rescue, as I very much hope you will."

On this occasion, unlike last time, she was not a member of

27

the public. So she drove on past the entrance to the public car park and up a short drive which ended in a walled entrance forecourt in front of the house. Garden chairs stood in one corner of the gravel, which seemed incongruous till the explanation dawned on her. This was the only outdoor area not open to sightseers. When the garden was full of paying customers it was the only place where the Lindsays could take the air in private.

Before she could ring the front door bell, Julian Lindsay appeared through a postern gate in the high wall of the entrance forecourt. "How kind of you to come, Mrs Grant. The others are through in the Lily Court, it's this way."

He led her through the gate and locked it after them, for this was the frontier between the garden and the Lindsays' private domain. The gate opened into a small enclosure shaded by the north wall of the house, containing a typical Jekyll "garden picture" of contrasting foliage, with a few phloxes and late lilies growing up through ferns. An archway at the other end opened into the Lily Court, where Mary Lindsay was standing beside the pool looking as dishevelled as ever. Beside her was another woman in her sixties, with aggressively tidy clothes, black boot-button eyes and an air of authority. Julian introduced her as "Barbara Seymour, an old friend and neighbour of ours who has kindly agreed to join the board of trustees".

Forewarned about this during Julian's phone call, Celia had looked up Barbara Seymour in *Who's Who* and discovered a brilliant Cambridge degree and a meteoric career in the wartime and post-war Civil Service, followed by a stretch as headmistress of one of England's most prestigious boarding schools for girls. Now retired, she had served on Royal Commissions and other report-producing bodies, and few social or educational problems seemed to have escaped her attention. She was a Justice of the Peace and a C.B.E., though there was no longer a British Empire for her to be a Commander of. The only recreations confessed to in her *Who's Who* entry were chess and bridge.

A glance at Julian's entry had shown that he and Barbara

28

had been Cambridge contemporaries, at Christ's and Girton respectively; and that his progress up the ladder of various ministries connected with trade and industry had been far less meteoric than hers up the Ministry of Transport.

"We all hope you'll agree to join us, Mrs Grant," said Julian.

"As I told you, I'll have to think carefully about it," said Celia. "It's a question of finding the time."

"Finding the time for voluntary work is always a problem, isn't it?" said Barbara Seymour in a voice thick with creamy committee woman's malice. Her mouth was smiling but the boot-button eyes were not. Finding time is a simple matter of organization, the eyes seemed to say, but probably too difficult for a little goose like you; moreover (as the eyes swept downwards from Celia's face) you are absurdly overdressed.

This was true. Celia had dressed up to the nines to provide as great a contrast as possible to Saturday's spying female in a head-scarf and dark glasses. It seemed to have worked. Neither of the Lindsays showed any sign of recognition.

"This is the Lily Court, Mrs Grant," said Mary Lindsay with a wave towards the now tidied-up effigy of her brother. "She was so clever with the steps leading down to the water,* wasn't she? He loved this pool, I remember him sitting for hours on the seat there."

Celia made a mental note that in Mary Lindsay's conversation "he" meant Anthony Mortlock and "she" meant Gertrude Jekyll. The tour of the garden began and she followed the others out on to the great sweep of lawn behind the house. It looked quite different without the mob of sightseers. Unlike the formal gardens of great houses, this one had been designed for the enjoyment of a private family and came into its own without the shock of a noisy crowd. But as the tour went on through a mass of little enclosures, all making demands of gardeners' time,

*"I have always observed that a beautiful effect is gained by steps leading actually down into water. . . . Although steps are in the first place intended for the human foot, yet we have become so accustomed to them as an easy means of access from one level to another that in many cases they are also desirable as an aid to the eye, giving it the feeling of being invited to contemplate the lilies at its utmost ease." (G.J.)

Celia became more and more sorry for the Lindsays. This was the most labour-intensive garden she had ever seen, designed in the days when skilled gardeners were paid a pittance. Apart from gaps in borders attributable to the vandal with the weedkiller, there were faint signs of neglect everywhere. Monk's Mead could not be made manageable without changes and short cuts which would rob it of its authenticity as an historic garden. But its authenticity was its main attraction, without it it would be just another too-large garden struggling to survive.

"How marvellous of you to keep all this up, it must be slavery," she said.

"Ha!" exclaimed Barbara Seymour, on a note which implied that gardening on this scale was madness. Since the tour started she had worn a bewildered expression, like a visitor with no understanding of industrial processes being shown round a factory.

"You've never thought of giving it up?" Celia persisted.

"That's impossible for legal reasons," said Julian firmly.

"My parents and grandparents saw this garden through two world wars," Mary added. It was a rebuke. The idea was too shocking to discuss.

Celia asked if the admission charges, plus the income from the endowment, covered the costs.

"Almost, with the profit on the catering," said Mary eagerly, "and Julian makes up the rest out of his salary."

Celia had understood that Julian had retired, but found on enquiry that like many high civil servants he had been pounced on by a talent scout for private industry and offered a well-paid job with an electronics firm. He was on holiday, but it normally took him to London for four days a week.

In a Pink and Grey Garden, his dark, sharp-featured son Adam was dead-heading and tying in quickly and expertly. Celia steeled herself for awkward explanations as he was introduced to her, for he had seen much more of her than his parents as he shooed her away from the forbidden rubbish pit. But if he recognized her he gave no sign and went back to work at once with fierce concentration.

They moved on into the Blue Garden, where the delphiniums were over and despite some blue campanulas and much pulling about of blue clematis the dominant note was struck by pale yellow oenotheras and hollyhocks.

"Your Blue Garden isn't very blue, is it," said Barbara Seymour on a fault-finding note.

"Why should it be?" snapped Mary. "Surely you know she* always said blue needed a contrast to set it off?"

How did Barbara manage not to know that, if she was such a close friend of the family? What was a horticultural illiterate doing on the board of trustees of an historic garden? Mary had ticked her off quite viciously, the "close friendship" must be with Julian, not with her.

As they strolled up the ravaged Long Borders it was impossible to pretend not to have noticed the gaps. *No Hydrangeas for Miss Jekyll*, Celia thought irreverently, or at least, not enough. Aloud she said: "D'you get much trouble with vandalism?"

"Horrors, yes," said Mary in a shocked voice. "It's always bad in August, that's the only month when really nasty people visit gardens."

Barbara glared at Celia to convey that she had committed a *gaffe*. "You're trampling on sensitive ground," she hissed in an undertone. "Don't ask her any more, Julian will explain."

Julian and Barbara exchanged glances. There seemed to be an understanding between them that Mary had to be treated as a psychiatric case. While Barbara kept her attention occupied Julian told Celia what she knew already; people who believed Mary guilty of practising euthanasia on her mother were damaging the garden to punish her; anyone who knew her would find the accusation incredible, but she was morbidly sensitive about it and terrified that news of the vandalism might leak into the press.

*"People will sometimes spoil some garden project for the sake of a word. For instance a Blue Garden may be hungering for a group of white lilies, or for something of palest lemon yellow, but is not allowed to have it because it is called the Blue Garden and there must be no flowers in it but blue flowers. Surely the business of the Blue Garden is to be beautiful as well as blue." (G.J.)

31

"How beastly for you, I am sorry," said Celia. "What sort of people are they?"

"Religious fanatics, we imagine. Some of these obscure sects are very violent. Last week they defaced her brother's statue, a specially cruel thing to do, because she was deeply attached to him."

"Dear me. How did that happen?"

"It was very well organized. Our son Adam was on watch in the Lily Court, we have to police the place when the garden's crowded. He saw a woman acting suspiciously in the Wild Garden and went after her but she was a decoy, to get him away from the Lily Court and the statue."

Julian's description of the mysterious woman disguised in a head-scarf and dark glasses interested Celia greatly. What interested her even more was that it was impossible to see into the Wild Garden from the Lily Court.

There was a gap, she saw now, between the backs of the Long Borders and the walls covered with climbing plants behind them; not a regular path but a space wide enough for anyone working the back of the border to get a barrow along. She decided that most of the damage had been done from there. It would be easy to creep along behind the tall plants, using a sprayer with a long lance. But how would a visitor to the garden get a sprayer with a long lance past the vigilance of the Lindsays and their staff? Had the spraying been done at night? Difficult to see what one was doing. In the evening, perhaps, after work in the garden had stopped. The perimeter fence was wire mesh, but not too high to climb over.

"Could anyone on your staff be involved in the vandalism?" Celia asked.

"No, that's out of the question. We close the garden on Mondays, it's their day off and that's when most of the damage seems to happen. A month ago someone got in while we were out and cut down, believe it or not, a *Magnolia macrophylla*, a marvellous tree; they couldn't have chosen anything more heartbreaking."

"Then it must have been someone who knew a bit about rare

trees."

"Perhaps, but one can't start suspecting one's staff or life would become intolerable."

"They've all been with you a long time?"

He either failed to hear the question or did not choose to, and launched into a disquisition about Gertrude's use of variegated maize as a foliage plant in herbaceous borders. Further up the Long Borders the gardener with the cleft chin was poking in brushwood supports, none too soon, among pentstemons that threatened to collapse.

"Morning George, lovely day." said Julian.

George was not in the mood to agree that the day was lovely. He began grumbling about shortage of staff, and in particular the absence of someone called Martin, without whom he could not manage. Mary made a mock-terrified face and hurried Celia away. "He keeps threatening to give us the push, it frightens the life out of me, let's leave Julian to pacify him."

She moved on to where two youngish gardeners were filling a devastated area of the border with geraniums in a cruel shade of pink, and bright yellow African marigolds.* Mary watched one of them break the main stem of a geranium as he unpotted it. "Oh, do be careful Bert," she said, and added when they were out of earshot: "It's dreadful, you have to watch them all the time, but they were all we could get. I'm not taking you into the Wild Garden. The Munstead Strain primroses are a disgrace, I'm ashamed to show them to you. They should have been divided last June, but we got behind and I thought the autumn would do and then all the gardeners left and we couldn't get anyone for weeks. By the time we'd hired more staff Julian had fallen downstairs at his London flat and I had him in bed for a month. And before we got properly organized again Mother had died and we never really caught up."

Celia sympathized and asked why the gardeners had left in a body. The explanation seemed not to be sinister. Wages at

*"There are among geraniums some of a raw magenta pink that I regret to see in many gardens, and that will certainly never be admitted into mine . . . the full yellow African marigold has to my eye a raw quality that I am glad to avoid." (G.J.)

Monk's Mead were not princely, and it so happened that one by one they had been offered more money elsewhere.

Julian joined them again and they started back through the range of theme gardens towards the house. As they entered the October Garden someone ran out of it at the other end. "Who was that?" cried Mary nervously.

"Only Tessa," said Julian.

"But there was someone with her, a man." Mary hurried on into the Gold Garden, with Julian trailing after her.

"Who's Tessa?" Celia asked Barbara.

"The grand-daughter. In her second year at Cambridge. Not a bad brain, but very difficult. Normally lives with her mother who's a hopeless neurotic but she's here with Adam for the summer."

"He's divorced then?"

"Five years ago. Carol led him a frightful dance. Adam fixed Tessa up with a summer job helping with teas down in the barn. The theory was that they should get to know each other better."

"Has it not worked out?"

Barbara made a gloomy face. "They're both prickly, defensive people."

They had moved on out of the labyrinth of theme gardens into the pergola with the wisteria along it. The vista at the end was closed by a pleasant little building; a former gardener's cottage, Barbara explained, which Adam had moved into when he married.

Mary was rattling the knocker on the cottage door. "They went in here," she stormed. "It's locked, and he's in there with her."

"Who is?" asked Julian.

"You know perfectly well who, I told her never to bring him here again."

She continued her attack on the door. It was flung open by a furious young woman who shouted: "What the hell d'you think you're doing, Gran, storming the Bastille?"

She was tall and striking-looking, with curly black hair, her father's well-chiselled features and very blue eyes, a raving beauty in fact. Peering out from behind her was a gangling young man in granny-glasses with a pale, studious face.

"Tessa, how dare you bring him here?" cried Mary.

This promised to be interesting, but Celia was not allowed to take it in. Barbara Seymour dragged her aside by force. "Your husband worked at Kew, I understand," she began loudly. "I suppose you picked up what you know about gardening from him."

Despite much practice at listening to one conversation while conducting another, Celia was too fascinated by what she was overhearing to explain at all clearly that, on the contrary, she had a Master of Science degree in Horticulture from a respectable agricultural college. As far as she could make out, a four-sided confrontation was going on behind her. Mary was ordering Julian to march the young man off the premises and calling him a "dirty little weasel of a Peeping Tom". Tessa was ordering the young man to stand firm and accusing her grandparents of all the bourgeois sins in the Marxist calendar. There was a lot that Celia missed, and by the time Barbara released her the argument had descended to the prosaic level of how the young man in the granny-glasses was to get back to the station.

"Crawling on all fours in a hair shirt with his tail between his legs?" Tessa snarled, "or how?"

"Adam can drive him," Mary decided.

"Okay, come on Peter before they put you in their gas chamber," Tessa snapped, and led him away to find her father.

"Go with them, Barbara, will you?" said Mary, "and make sure he really goes."

Barbara raised her eyebrows significantly at Julian, and went.

"Julian, is it true, what Tessa said?" Mary asked.

"Is what true in that farrago of nonsensical accusations?"

"That you didn't fall downstairs. She says you were mugged, and told people you'd fallen downstairs because being mugged is undignified."

"Tessa's allegation is partly true and partly untrue. I was

35

mugged in the street and kept quiet about it, but not from the motive she attributes to me."

"Then why? Why didn't you tell me?"

"Obviously because I thought it would worry you," said Julian, not at all kindly. "Can we talk about something else?"

"No, I'm very upset, you should have — oh no!" She broke off. An expensively dressed woman with a guide book had appeared at the far end of the pergola and heads were bobbing beyond the hedges of the theme gardens. "Horrors, it can't be opening time already? Mrs Grant — "

The accompanying gesture was an appeal to Celia to go. She let Julian guide her back to the gate in the wall which separated the public part of the garden from the entrance courtyard where she had left her car.

"This damage by vandals is very worrying," she said. "You've thought of guard dogs?"

"To satisfy the legal and insurance requirements we'd have to instal a higher perimeter fence. The cost would be prohibitive." He unlocked the door in the wall and let her through. "I do hope you've decided to join the board?" he said, and opened the car door for her.

Celia's mind was split. Half of it said "not on your nelly, the problems of this garden terrify me." The other half answered "but what a fascinating problem, and I can always resign when I've solved it."

Aloud, she muttered something about not being sure how much use she would be.

"Oh, having you would be a tremendous help. Graham Harrison's right, we're too close to it all, we can't see the wood for the trees. An outside view from an experienced horticulturist like yourself would be immensely valuable, do say 'yes'."

"My solicitor will want to know what responsibilities I'm letting myself in for," she said. "Send me a photocopy of the trust deed to show him, and if he okays it I'll have a go."

"What did you make of her, Mary?"

"I don't know, she seems a harmless little thing. Julian, how could

36

Tessa do it? She knows what he's after and why we don't want him here."

"It's tiresome of her, I agree. Try not to let it upset you too much."

"Adam must talk to her, he's her father, she might listen. Get him to look in here when he's had his lunch."

"Very well, my dear. You're not eating your sandwich."

"I don't want it. I'm prostrate with exhaustion, I shall lie down upstairs for ten minutes before we have to go out again. Send Adam up to me when he comes."

". . . Coffee, Barbara?"

"Please. She's cracking up."

"I don't think it's serious, not more than one would expect in the circumstances. What did you make of the Grant woman?"

"For once I agree with Mary. Not much there, don't you think? She seems to have some sort of qualification from an agricultural college, but that sort of thing doesn't amount to an intellectual discipline, does it? What did you think?"

"I don't think she'll be a problem, and if we take her on at least it will stop Harrison fussing."

Celia ate her toasted sandwich and drank her coffee. On leaving Julian she had driven no further than the customers' car park at the public entrance to Monk's Mead. She intended to shop in Guildford on her way home, which meant picking up a snack lunch somewhere, so what was wrong with the Monk's Mead barn, where refreshment could be combined with another look at the Lindsays' beautiful but insubordinate grand-daughter?

There was nothing wrong with the toasted sandwich except its price, and the place was obviously well run. Competent village ladies manned a well-stocked self-service counter. The walls had been used to create a Gertrude Jekyll shrine, with a reproduction of Sir William Nicholson's painting, in the Tate Gallery, of her gardening boots, and blown-up photographs of her garden at Munstead Wood. Celia often wished that colour photography had been invented earlier. Munstead Wood looked rather messy in black and white.

Tessa and another girl were collecting dirty crockery abandoned on the tables and taking it away to the washing-up machine. The place was full and they were very busy. Celia wondered what she had hoped to discover by coming here to eat. The other girl was a complete contrast to dark and vital Tessa, and repaid study. She was pale and thin, a washed out blonde with grey smudges of fatigue under her eyes, an anorexia case if Celia had ever seen one. She was much slower on the job than Tessa and kept watching the door as if expecting someone.

While she was out at the back with a trolley-load of crockery a thin young man with a two-day growth of black beard came in. Instead of joining the queue for the counter he stood in the middle of the room staring round. When the blonde girl reappeared from the kitchen he looked at her gloomily and said "Hi, Annie."

Annie gave a gasp of dismay, abandoned her trolley and fled into the back premises.

"Hey, come back," he called.

The village ladies behind the counter showed resigned disgust at this development, as if it had happened many times before. It was left to Tessa to take charge.

"So you're here again," she said, marching up to him.

"I want to talk to Annie."

"Listen, you creepy little nuisance. Annie doesn't want to talk to you, she's told you over and over. And now she's locked herself into the grotty staff convenience and won't come out till you've gone, which had better be damn soon because I'm not doing her bloody work for her with you stuck there in everyone's way like a poisonous little male chauvinist toadstool, so, unless you want me to borrow a rolling pin from Mrs Hawkins here and lam you in your pathetic little balls with it, you'd better go now."

"But listen, Miss . . ."

"Out. Shoo. Away with you into outer space. Scram."

He began to give ground before her onrush, but not fast enough to satisfy her. With a few rapid judo-like movements she pinioned his arms behind his back and frog-marched him out. "And stay out," she shouted, landing a shrewd kick on his

38

bottom.

The customers had just time to settle down again to their meal, and Celia to decide that her observation post was proving interesting after all, when Adam Lindsay walked in, grasped Tessa's arm and said something in a low voice.

"No, damn it, leave me alone!" cried Tessa as she freed herself and walked on.

He stood there looking after her with a lost expression. The tea-barn seemed to be an unlucky place for men. As he turned to go he caught Celia's eye and came over to her table. "Hullo. It was you in the head-scarf and dark glasses."

"Yes. Thank you for not embarrassing me by making an issue of it in front of your parents. I thought I'd have a look round before I got too involved."

"Good idea. Was I very rude?"

"No, firm but tactful. How clever of you to spot me nosing around that rubbish pit. You can't see into the Wild Garden from where you were in the Lily Court."

"No. One of the gardeners told me he'd seen someone rummaging about there and said I ought to investigate."

"Which gardener was it?" Celia asked.

"Bert, I think, or it may have been Ted, one of the young ones anyway. Why d'you ask?"

"I just wondered."

He looked amused. "Really? Why did you 'just wonder'? No, on second thoughts don't bother to explain, tell me whether you've decided to join the board."

"I'm not quite sure," said Celia. She was already regretting her impulsive 'yes' to Julian and wondering how to get out of it.

"Do join us, we need an outside viewpoint. I just prune and dead head and weed like crazy, slogging along from day to day, there's no time to think about the long-term problems."

"Or is it that thinking about them frightens you?"

His smile was a taut grimace, which did not necessarily mean amusement. Without answering, he rose. "I must get back on patrol. Excuse me."

So one of the gardeners had told him, Celia thought as she

39

watched him go. He had to be got away from the Lily Court while the sinister tableau was mounted round the statue, but anyone wandering about in the Wild Garden would do as the basis for an exaggerated account of suspicious goings-on near the sensitive rubbish pit. Did it follow that Bert, or possibly Ted, was responsible for the vandalism? No. Gardener A tells gardener B to alert Adam Lindsay, who as a member of the family has the clout to deal firmly with misbehaviour.

But the day's discoveries included far more interesting morsels of food for thought, and she began to chew over them.

Back in the autumn the four gardeners employed at Monk's Mead had all been offered better wages elsewhere. Coincidence? Or did someone have a motive for wanting to infiltrate replacements?

At roughly the same time (another coincidence?) Julian had been beaten up in London so badly that he had been in bed for a month. He had lied about being mugged, and claimed to have fallen downstairs. To avoid alarming his wife, or was there another motive?

And here was another puzzle, about Julian's attitude to the vandalism. By every test of means and opportunity the gardeners were the obvious suspects. They had access to the garden when it was closed, to spraying equipment and to weedkiller. Yet Julian maintained that the vandals went to work on Mondays, when the garden was closed to the public and the gardeners had the day off and were elsewhere. But weedkiller damage would only become obvious after a time lag which varied according to the weather and the strength of the chemical used, there was no means of establishing exactly when it had been applied. If the critical day was Monday, as Julian alleged, why did the family go out on a Monday and leave the garden unguarded, as they had done on the day when the magnolia was cut down? Why was the use of guard dogs ruled out? They did not have to be savage Alsatians roaming loose within a high perimeter fence. Ordinary dogs chained up at strategic points would bark at strangers and raise the alarm.

Why did Julian insist that the gardeners were above

suspicion? Why had he not taken the obvious precautions which would exclude everyone but the gardeners? Why was he directing suspicion away from them by having the garden ostentatiously patrolled during opening hours? He was refusing to face facts about them that stared him in the face. Why?

During his years in the Civil Service he must have spent much time advising his Minister that the options open to him were policies A, B, and C, all of which would have disastrous consequences, but that on balance the disaster produced by policy C was preferable to the others. Had that habit of thought persisted? Had he decided, on balancing the pros and cons at Monk's Mead, that suspect gardeners were preferable to no gardeners, and therefore should not be sacked at the height of the gardening season when replacements could not be had for love or money?

This seemed to Celia a barely credible explanation, and another suspicion began to take shape in her mind. The replacement gardeners had been infiltrated and Julian's hushed-up mugging had occurred *before old Mrs Mortlock's death*. What if the Lindsays' troubles had not been touched off by the inquest and the furore about euthanasia, but by some event long before that, back in the autumn?

What event? One that Julian knew about and had kept secret from his wife. He had lied to her about the mugging. He could not afford to admit that the gardeners might be vandals, because they had been infiltrated before the event that was supposed to have caused the vandalism. Julian knew why he had been beaten up in the street and why the garden was being slowly reduced to a ruin. But he was letting his wife suffer the agony of believing it was all directed against her. Suddenly Celia was enormously angry on Mary Lindsay's behalf and determined to do something about it.

Horrors, what a nasty kettle of fish, she thought as she drove out of the Monk's Mead car park. Were the noose and the piglet part of a separate operation directed against Mary? If not, where did they fit in? And an enormous field of speculation had opened up on another subject: who had given Mrs Mortlock the

41

sleeping pills and why?

Halfway into Guildford to do her shopping, a speeding police car passed her going in the opposite direction.

It was on its way to investigate a report that a man had been murdered in the garden at Monk's Mead.

THREE

"Hɪ Tʜᴇʀᴇ Gᴇᴏʀɢᴇ. Who is he then?"

"Dunno. No clue to identity among personal effects."

"Let's have a look at him. Age, say forty-five. Balding. Reddish hair, corpulent build. Cause of death, kitchen knife between shoulder blades. Trousers wet in the crutch. Pissed himself, has he?"

"S'right. You would, with that thing stuck in you."

"You asked the family who he is?"

"They say they dunno, never seen him before."

"What's he doing lying here by their front door then?"

"They say they dunno. This bit's not open to the public, they say."

"Slipped in through that door in the wall, most likely. Which leads to where?"

"A little yard with bushes in."

"Which is open to the public?"

"That's right. It's like a maze through there, little open-air rooms sort of, opening out of each other, each with different coloured flowers in. The door's not locked, he could have slipped in through it easy without being seen."

"Anyone checked on that?"

"Chris is out there now. He's got them all on the lawn, there's hordes of them, finding out if anyone saw anything."

"Who found him?"

"Sir Julian."

"Alone?"

"I'm not sure. When I arrived Lady L. was out here too, carrying on a bit."

"And they both say they don't know who he is? Pockets?"

"One entry ticket to garden. Small change. No wallet. He'd have left it in his jacket in the car."

43

"Hell, so we wait till they shut for the night and see which car's left over. Look George, you wait here for forensic while I talk to Sir Julian."

Back at Archerscroft Nurseries, Celia rang Graham Harrison to say that unless her solicitor made difficulties she was willing to replace him on the board of trustees. But it was not news to him.

"Sir Julian rang me with the glad tidings this morning, shortly after you left him. I'm sure your solicitor won't raise any objection, there's no personal liability involved for the trustees."

"I'd like to have a long talk with you," said Celia, "about the problems at Monk's Mead and how you think they could be solved."

"I'd be delighted, but could we leave it for a few weeks? You see, I've been postponing a trip I want to make until this business was settled, and now I'm off. I've never been to the Holy Land, and I thought I'd remedy the omission while I can still walk after a fashion."

Damn, an excuse if ever I heard one, Celia thought. What did Harrison know and why was he unwilling to tell? She walked out crossly into the frame yard, where Bill Wilkins was pricking out seedlings of *Euphorbia mellifera*. As a head gardener he would be perfect, she decided as she started the evening watering, but for the transistor radio blaring out pop from the local station. But the pop had just been interrupted by what sounded like disc jockey's chatter. Bill had stopped work to listen, which was unusual. It must be a news flash.

When the music started again he switched it off and strolled over to her. "Oh Celia, you'll hop and curse when you hear what you missed out on. Someone's been murdered at Monk's Mead."

"How extraordinary. I was there this morning."

"Now Celia. I know it's hard, a lovely corpse and you not there with your magnifying glass but we haven't the time, we're much too busy, so don't you go galloping off there."

"I wouldn't dream of it, murders horrify me. It's just that

44

when they happen near to me I have to know. Tell me at once, who's killed who?"

"An unidentified man has been stabbed by persons unknown."

Celia, who had been wondering whether Mary Lindsay had strangled her grand-daughter or *vice versa*, abandoned this scenario in favour of Sir Julian stabbing a religious maniac armed with a garden spray. When she surfaced from these thoughts, Bill was watching her with a worried expression.

"Celia, just think how much we got to do between now and Christmas. I know you're frantic with curiosity, but you must keep away from that place."

"I can't altogether. I've said I'd be a trustee there."

"You can still back out."

"I'd look a bit of a heel if I ratted now when they're in trouble."

"Then be a trustee and see they keep the weeds down and their fingers out of the cashbox, but don't prance around helping the police with their enquiries, because — "

The bell on the outside wall of the office interrupted him with its clamour. A belated customer was ringing for attention.

"We're closed," said Celia. "Better see who it is, though."

Bill peered over the hedge. "Police car," he reported. "Now don't you help them with their enquiries more than you have to, because the girls have all gone home and there's a lot of watering still do do."

Fortunately from the time-saving point of view, the police were also in a hurry to complete their "routine enquiries" and get away home. They were mainly interested in when she had left Monk's Mead and whether or not the door had been locked between the public part of the garden and the entrance courtyard where she had left her car.

"It's kept locked," she said. "I remember Sir Julian unlocking it to let me through."

"And re-locking it afterwards on the courtyard side?"

"Yes. I remember thinking how awful it must be to have to take that sort of precautions."

45

"Just one other thing, Mrs Grant. During your tour of the garden with Sir Julian and party, did anything strike you as unusual, anything that might help us? Or was it all quite normal?"

"Well, both the Lindsays were rather on edge, because of this worrying problem with vandalism in the garden. They must have told you about that."

"Yes. Apart from that, there was no unusual incident?"

Celia hesitated. What about the extraordinary panic caused by the discovery that Tessa's disapproved-of boy friend had infiltrated through the defences into Monk's Mead? Should she mention it? No, it was probably irrelevant, something to do with elderly shock at the sexual *mores* of the liberated young. Why involve the unfortunate Tessa in embarrassed explanations about that?

"I can't think of anything that would help you," she said, "but if I may ask a question, has the victim been identified yet? It could even be someone I know."

"I doubt it, Mrs Grant. We've established from his passport that he's a French national. He was a member of a coach tour that came over from France, and of course he was missing when the coach was ready to leave."

"Now George, let's run over what we got. Antoine Robelin, age forty-six, nationality French, profession, according to his passport, Notaire, which is some kind of lawyer. Member of coach party which set out three days ago from Béthune, which is in northern France somewhere near Lille. Home address, gawd, I can't pronounce that, but it's a mining village not far from Béthune. You saw Mrs Grant? What did she say about that door?"

"He locked it again after letting her through."

"She's sure? How reliable as a witness?"

"Very, I'd say. Not a word too much, everything to the point."

"Interesting. When I asked Sir Julian whether he'd locked it he thought for a long time, then said he probably didn't."

"That's the safest answer for him. If two members of the public could have wandered in there to settle an argument quietly, that lets him out. What did you make of him?"

"Too smooth and controlled. Always thinks for a bit before he answers."

"Could be a habit those top people have, to show how carefully he's considered the question. I asked him if he thought the murder could be connected with this malicious damage they've been having in the garden. He goes broody for all of a minute before he says no, he's sure it's out of the question."

"If the malicious damage is religious maniacs rampaging because of Lady L's euthanasia like he says, he could be right. Deceased smelt a bit beery, beer doesn't go with religious mania."

"How about him for opportunity?"

"That's a bit dodgy too. He makes out he was never alone to do it. Okay, he says, Lady L. was having a headache upstairs and Adam, that's the son, went off somewhere after a bit, but Miss Seymour, remember her?"

"Friend of the family, that helped slap on the whitewash at the inquest? Used to be headmistress of that posh school?"

"That's her. According to Sir Julian she was still there when he comes out and finds that nasty bit of malicious damage lying on his doorstep."

"She'd gone by the time I got there."

"Yes. He says giving explanations to policemen with a corpse at her feet is not where an eminent lady who sits on Government commissions wishes to be seen. So she made herself scarce but remains at our disposal. Which means she'll back up Sir J. and say yes, she was there and no, he didn't stick a kitchen knife into anyone or she'd have noticed."

"Which could be true. Want me to see her?"

"Could you, George? I have to interview the coach party at their hotel, find out what they know about Robelin. It'll be a nightmare, with them all quacking away at that little twerp of an interpreter."

I want nothing to do with this murder, Celia told herself as she threw out the duds from a batch of a mimulus with unusual markings in the throat that she was raising. I wasn't there when it happened, thank goodness, and I have no wish to rush across the channel and investigate the background of a fat man hailing from that ugly, God-forsaken corner of northern France where world wars always begin; nor would I enjoy trudging along

47

canal banks *à la Maigret* and sniffing out earthy love affairs between Antoine Robelin the village *notaire* and the lock-keeper's wife. If there is a connection between the murder and the rest of the Monk's Mead problem, the police will find out soon enough.

But what about "the rest of the problem"? Mary Lindsay's distraught face haunted her. So helpless-looking a victim, bullied and deceived by her husband, must not be left in the lurch. But one could hardly take her aside and say "Look here, what's all this about?" She would clam up at once and tell Julian that the new member of the board was a nosy busybody. Nor could Celia say to her "I'm sure your husband's up to something sinister, but I don't know what and I can't prove it."

The thing would have to be approached from another angle: Tessa's. Why had Mary Lindsay's confrontation with her beautiful angry grand-daughter been so electric, and why had the sight of Tessa's boy friend with the granny-glasses sent Mary off into near-hysterics? There was also the washed-out blonde with anorexia whose rejected suitor had made a feeble sort of scene among the tables in the tea-barn. Tessa worked there too. The next step, clearly, was to pay the tea-barn another visit.

But Monk's Mead would be crawling with crime reporters plying their trade, interviewing anyone they could find about the murder. What would it look like if the new trustee was found ferreting away with the keenest of them, chatting up the tea-barn staff? From Celia's point of view the murder was a nuisance as well as a horrifying event. But an obvious solution presented itself: Bill must go.

"Me? Crikey, what for?"

"To chat up two young women in the tea-barn and ask them a question or two on my behalf."

"Why me?"

"They'll tell you things they wouldn't tell me."

"Oh I get it Celia. I'm to worm things out of them? I'm to fascinate them with me fatal beauty, is that it? Oh, Celia, you know how that caper always gets me into trouble."

48

Bill was a one-girl-friend man. But ever since his teens his absurd handsomeness had been landing him without warning in torrid situations not of his making and beyond his control.

"With two of them there's safety in numbers," she urged.

"You'd be surprised," said Bill gloomily.

"Come on, be a sport."

"I will not set meself up as a sex object to satisfy your morbid curiosity."

"Oh, really Bill, you're hysterical about this, you'll be burning your bra next. Besides, it's not curiosity. I'm desperately worried about Mary Lindsay, I think something awful might happen to her. Please don't argue. Go."

Bill looked at her set face and said "Okay Celia, what d'you want them asked?"

"George, guess what. You know how on a coach tour there's always a funny man, the one who tells bad jokes all the time and tries to make them sing and change hats and all that? Well, they say Robelin was the funny man."

"Life and soul of the party and general pain in the neck?"

"That's right, they were all fed up to the teeth with him by the time they got to Calais, and since then they've all been running a mile to get away from him whenever they could."

"Travelling by himself, was he?"

"That's right, and no one on the trip had ever met him before, nor do they ever want to meet him again."

"Tell you what, then. If you were using a coach tour as cover for something a bit wicked, the funny man everyone keeps clear of would be quite a good person to be."

It was late afternoon. Only a few customers were left in the barn at Monk's Mead. Tessa, magnificent in her dark fury, glowered at Bill across his tea table. "So what moronic thought-process gave you the bizarre idea that I'd want to have a drink with you?"

"Forget it then, if you don't want to. There's no need to have an epileptic fit about it."

49

"Such arrogance!" she stormed. "Why would I want to let myself be pawed in a pub by a pink-sugar sex-athlete with a designer hair-do who hopes I'll open my legs after two gin-and-tonics? I am not a damn sex object."

"Nor am I, you got sex on the brain," Bill blurted out, "so why don't you keep your legs and your mouth shut while I finish me tea."

"We're closing, so hurry up," said Tessa and stalked away.

Bill drank his tea hastily and prepared to leave. The other girl, the thin unappetizing blonde, was hovering by the exit in her outdoor things.

"You invited us both," she murmured as he passed her. "I'd like to come even if Tessa won't, if that's okay by you."

He could hardly refuse, but from his point of view it was far from okay, he'd have been safe with the two of them but to judge from the way this sad girl was looking at him he had exchanged Tessa's wounding frying pan for quite an ardent little fire.

"What's your name?" he asked as they strolled towards the van.

"Ann. Most people call me Annie."

"Mine's Bill. What's biting your friend?"

"I'll tell you when we get to the Six Bells. That's the nearest, out on the main road."

He put her in the van and drove off. Half way down the lane they met a man on a bicycle coming up. Annie made a startled movement, but checked it quickly and said nothing.

"What's wrong then?" Bill asked.

"Nothing . . . ."

He glanced in the mirror. The man had got off the bicycle and was staring after them.

Annie's silence lasted till they were installed behind, respectively, a beer and a sweet sherry in the bar of the Six Bells.

"I hope you don't mind me saying I'd come," she began, "and don't be alarmed, I shan't fling myself at your feet in a romantic agony and say 'take me'."

"That's fine then, Annie," said Bill, not entirely reassured.

"It was intellectual curiosity really, I've always wondered

what it would feel like to go out with a really smashing man and watch all the women looking at him and wondering what on earth he saw in a washed-out blonde with a bad complexion like me. Don't look now, but it's happening all round us, I'm enjoying it a lot."

Embarrassed and surprised, Bill choked into his beer.

"Now we've cleared that point up," she continued, "let's get down to business. What d'you want to know?"

"Why d'you think I'm after information?"

She chuckled. "What could you be but a news man, coming into the tea-barn and chatting Tessa and me up in that heavy way? There's been hordes of them in there ever since the murder, you're at the back of the queue. I didn't tell them anything though, Sir Julian's ordered us not to talk to the media."

"But you're going to talk to me?"

"That's right, I'm making you an exception, in exchange for having every woman in this bar goggling at me. Go on, question me. If I know the answer I'll tell you."

"Okay then, let's start with the gloomy bloke in the corner, the one with the dark shave that just came in."

"What about him?"

"He passed us in the lane on his bicycle, he's followed us in here, and he's staring at you like a lovesick dormouse. Who is he?"

"No idea, I've never seen him before."

"Oh Annie, that's not true, I bet you have. You're a pair, you and Tessa. What got into her, biting me fingers off like that?"

"That's easy, it's her idea of fun. She got bored with telling the media that she's not allowed to talk to them, so she started giving them her chauvinist pig routine instead."

"She's in bad with her grandparents. What about?"

Annie drew back. "That's cheating. You're only supposed to ask about the murder."

"Oh come on now. Tell me."

"No. Tessa's private affairs have nothing to do with it."

"If you tell me, I'll give you ever such a sexy look and let you

51

hold me hand and we'll drive the women there mad."

"My God, stop leering like that, they'll think you're a pimp recruiting me for a cabaret in Buenos Aires."

"Come on, tell me about Tessa's boy friend, the brainy looking one in glasses."

"You mean Peter Barton?"

"Is that his name? Why do her parents hate him so?"

"They think he's only her boy-friend for what he can get out of her."

"Money?"

"No. Family secrets."

"Are there any?"

"Must be. Otherwise why would they be so terrified of him?"

"Funny set-up," said Bill. "Why does he want to know their family secrets?"

"Because he's a post-graduate student at her college in Cambridge and he's researching a thesis on the poetry of Anthony Mortlock."

"Hi, George. Anything fresh come in?"

"Chris phoned about the keys to that door in the wall. All the Lindsays have one, that's Sir Julian and Lady, and the son and the grand-daughter who's doing a summer job in the tea-barn."

"Could anyone have borrowed a key and had it copied?"

"Chris asked Sir Julian that. He thought a bit and said on the one hand yes and on the other hand no."

"Having it both ways as usual. Anything else?"

"Oh yes, there was. Chris says a knife similar to the murder weapon is missing from the kitchen at the tea barn."

"How fascinating," said Celia when Bill reported back to her on his conversation with Annie. "Did you ask her again about the man with the dark shave?"

"Sure. She won't talk about him, but she knows him, I bet. He must be the one came moaning after her in the tea room."

"A boy friend she's had a row with?" Celia suggested.

"One she gave the push to, more likely. I was dead scared at

52

first, what's she after, I thought, crikey what's going to happen? But she was okay in the end."

"Okay" had a special meaning in Bill's private language. As a result of many hair-raising experiences he divided humanity into two classes. The sexually continent who left him alone, were "okay". The liable to run amok were not. Among the alarmingly non-okay were middle-aged women who could not resist the temptation to run their fingers through his hair, teenage girls who threw off their clothes without being invited to do so, men of all ages who suddenly revealed unexpected tendencies, others with even more bizarre ways of embarrassing him. Annie had refrained from doing any of those things and had also produced some useful information. According to her the problem of how to deal with the vandal attack on the garden had produced a rift in the family. Adam had wanted to call in the police, Mary had protested that this would mean publicity and she would die of shame, and her husband had supported her. Adam had then backed down like a dutiful son, whereupon Tessa exploded in a whirlwind of anger.

"Annie says Tessa has funny ideas," Bill reported. "Like believing in something they call 'the conspiracy theory of society', what's that?"

"She believes that when things go wrong, it's the result of a deep-laid government plot and not, as I do, of the chronic chaos in the corridors of power."

"That's right then, that fits in with what Annie said. Tessa thinks everything should be let hang out, all the dirty washing, and nothing kept secret, then there'd be no problems because people would see who was up to the dirty business and stop it. Annie says Tessa told her gran that. Call in the police, she said, let them stop beating up the blacks and do something useful for a change, tell everyone there's religious maniacs wrecking the garden and to hell with anyone who says you poisoned your mother. That made them all hit the roof, and there was a lot of shouting and effing and beeing among the hydrangeas. Celia, what's an 'emasculated Orpheus-figure'?"

"I'm not sure till I know the context."

53

"Tessa says this Anthony Mortlock that wrote the poems has been made to look like one, it's all part of this idea of hers of getting the dirt all out in the open. She says Anthony's mum, that's old Mrs Mortlock that died of the sleeping pills, right? She got a man to write a book about him, a memoir they called it, only she told him what to put in, which was a lovey-dovey mum's eye view, and what to leave out, which was the naughty bits."

"Oh, splendid, what are the naughty bits?"

"Annie doesn't know, but Tessa says they aren't dead naughty, just things that would make him look like a man instead of an emasculated what's-it. And she says a lot of people know what he was really like, including this Peter Barton who's doing research on him, and it's all going to come out in the end so why not now?"

"But Lady Lindsay doesn't agree?"

"No way does she agree, she had a fit when Tessa brought boy-friend Barton to see her with his notebook. The way I look at it, Tessa's gran knows some naughty things about brother Anthony that Tessa doesn't. Better get hold of this memoir tomorrow, eh Celia? See what's been put in, so you can guess what dirty bits the old lady got left out."

"They sell the book in the barn at Monk's Mead," Celia said. "I bought one when I was there yesterday."

But on dipping into it she had found it too sentimental to stomach and had put it aside in disgust. When Bill had gone she picked it up again with fresh interest. "The Collected Poems of Anthony Mortlock," she read from the title page, "with a Memoir by Andrew Stamford, D.Litt., based on Materials Supplied by His Mother."

It was a mother's eye view and no mistake. Even in infancy little Anthony had shown a passionate love for natural beauty, watching with entranced eyes as the trailing plumes of the wisteria moved in the breeze on the pergola above his pram. . . . His blameless boyhood and clean-limbed youth were dealt with in the same rose-tinted style, with heavy emphasis on his delight in the "enchanted" garden at Monk's Mead.

Imbedded in the morass of sentiment were the essential facts. Winchester, then St Saviour's College Oxford with a scholarship in Modern Languages. An outstanding academic career, testified to by a quote to that effect by his tutor, plus charm, social success and athletic prowess, on the authority of quotes by friends and contemporaries. A brilliant degree, followed by a year of post-graduate research in Germany where he meets Julian Lindsay, who shares his distaste for the disgusting Nazi carry-on and becomes a close friend. Then comes the Second World War, whereupon our hero joins the Air Force and performs as brilliantly as ever on hush-hush Intelligence work, nature not specified, for which his fluent command of German qualifies him uniquely. Quotation of tribute from a colleague to this alleged brilliance, nature of Intelligence work still not clear, for the book was published in 1948 when such matters were still hush-hush and the intelligence pundits had not begun writing inaccurate reminiscences in which they leaked like baskets.

Some time during all this, arrival on the scene of girl friend, clearly approved of by Mrs Mortlock ("though there was no formal engagement, they knew in their hearts . . . etc.") Long quote of reminsicences by girl friend, name not given, she is referred to throughout as "K——". But brave and upright Anthony becomes increasingly guilt-ridden because he is sitting being brilliant in the safety of a requisitioned English country house while others die for their country. One evening he comes home to Monk's Mead in a brainstorm of despair. He can stand it no longer, he has shaken the country-house dust off his feet and intends to join a combatant unit as a private soldier. He must do this, he says, under an assumed name, because people with high-level secret knowledge are not allowed to risk being captured, in case they tell all to a German interrogator. It will be better, therefore, if his parents do not know his name or the name of his unit, because they will have to answer enquiries about him when he is posted as a deserter. But they can assure the enquirers that he will die rather than betray his country's secrets.

Anthony then disappears from view, but they know he is still

55

in England because he telephones them and K—— at regular intervals. There is one last agonized meeting with K—— at "a seaside town in the north of England". Then the phone calls stop. After a tense wait, a letter arrives from the commanding officer of his unit, and here Celia has to hand it to Anthony for coming up to the standards of physical fitness and mental toughness needed for entry into an exclusive *corps d'élite*. The unit concerned is Number Four Commando. It has just taken part, the commanding officer says, in a cross-channel raid on Dieppe. When the time came to withdraw, Anthony was not in any of the landing craft. He was last seen swimming strongly, so there was still hope that he might have been taken prisoner.

His mother's enquiries through the Red Cross produced no news of him, and presently he was listed as "missing, presumed killed." Their only consolation was his commanding officer's remark that the Dieppe raid had produced "experience of combined operations which will be invaluable when the time comes to open a second front in Europe".

Enclosed with the commanding officer's letter was an envelope addressed to Anthony's mother, marked "to be forwarded in the event of my death". It contained his will, and the poem urging her to "shed no tears for him" from which the verse was quoted on the plinth of his statue in the garden.

Celia had been making a mental list of questions as she read. What was the high-level Intelligence work? How cast-iron was "missing, presumed killed"? Who was the girl friend? Was guilt about his non-combatant status the real cause of his brainstorm of despair? The Lindsays — Anthony's sister married to his close friend — must know anything there was to know, what were the skeletons they were pushing back so busily into cupboards? Who was this Andrew Stamford who had written the memoir? Was he still alive? What would he have written if Mrs Mortlock had not been standing over him with a shotgun forcing him to turn her darling boy into a whitewashed plaster saint?

Having digested the Memoir Celia turned to the Collected Poems. They were in chronological order, starting with

schoolboy efforts which a charitable critic would call promis-
ing. These were followed by maturer poems which Celia
thought rather good, particularly one contrasting the romantic
luxuriance of a garden at night, perhaps the Wild Garden at
Monk's Mead, with the orderly precision of the "clockwork
stars" in the cloudless sky above it.

Presently she came on a love poem:

TO K—— ON OUR ANNIVERSARY

When my secret hand met yours
And we stole that first shy kiss
Did I guess what hidden doors
Lay beyond that sweet new bliss?

Did I know what treasure store
As we opened mind to mind
Waited for me to explore
Or what riches I would find?

I tremble, as your sleeping head
Lies against my grateful heart.
I would be as good as dead
If our hands had stayed apart.

This was the simplest and most direct of the love poems, but
there were plenty more, all tacitly or explicitly addressed to
K——, and a shadowy picture of her began to emerge. She was
dark-haired, with a classic profile which reminded Anthony, he
said, of:

"Some burnished coin of the antique South."

whereas the grave tones of her voice:

"Echoed a sea-cave's solemn melody."

It was clear that the relationship had involved a happy meeting
of minds, adding an extra dimension to a love affair. Anthony,
with a respectable academic record of his own, kept stressing

57

that he admired her for her brains as well as her beauty. Celia decided that she was probably an older woman. He was born in 1918, so she would be well into her seventies now if she was still alive.

Searching through the book Celia came on a poem entitled "Highgate Cemetery" which wove decorative phrases round a grave from which issued "wisdom's philosophic river", though the name of its bearded occupant was not mentioned. There were other poems of explicit ideological content; support for the communist struggle in Spain against the dictators, condemnation of the rearmament boom and the capitalist forces behind it, compassion for various classes of underdog. This was not surprising, he had simply absorbed the hopeful leftism which was the conventional wisdom of the universities in the run-up to the second world war. The verses of his last poem which were not quoted on his plinth were caustic about the appeasement of Hitler which had made the war possible.

But nothing had been said in the Memoir about his political attitudes, apart from a cagey reference to the "impatient idealism" of youth. Why not? What else had Mrs Mortlock censored? Celia lay awake for a long time, wondering.

FOUR

"I've examined the trust deed, Mrs Grant," said Celia's solicitor, "and there's no cause for concern about the point you raised. No personal liability falls on the trustees."

"Is there anything in it," she asked, "about what happens if the trust goes broke and the Lindsays decide to abandon the garden?"

"No, but there's a procedure laid down in the Act which would apply if, as you say, the trust failed because its aims were frustrated by circumstances."

"Are you sure? Sir Julian told me they couldn't close down the garden 'for legal reasons'."

"Really?" He looked at the papers in front of him again. "There's nothing here to that effect. . . . There was one thing that puzzled me, though. Yes, here it is. If the trust fails, the solicitors who acted for Mrs Mortlock in this matter have to be informed. They must also be informed of the deaths of Sir Julian or Lady Lindsay."

"Surely the family solicitors would know that sort of thing anyway?" Celia objected.

He looked at her oddly. "The family solicitors are Foster and King, down the street. This is a London firm."

"Dear me, how interesting. In other words, Mrs Mortlock left an instruction with them that she didn't want known locally. Something they have to do if the trust fails, or if either of the Lindsays dies."

"It is open to that interpretation, Mrs Grant, among others, but it couldn't affect the liability on the trustees. I have all the papers here, so we can go through the formalities now if you're

59

agreeable. Then it will be in order for you to attend the meeting of the trustees tomorrow morning."

"Think there's anything in it, George?"
"I dunno. What was the place called again?"
"Here we are. Bruay-en-Artois. It's ten kilometres from the place we can't pronounce where Robelin lived. That's quite a distance."
"But it's the only lead we got. Pass it on to the French, do we?"
"Sure, let them run around a bit in their funny hats. They're getting bloody nowhere, like us."

Celia arrived at Monk's Mead in good time for the meeting. She parked her car in the entrance court, then realized with a shock that she was stepping out on to gravel occupied only a week ago by a dead Frenchman with a knife protruding from his back.

No noise came from the public part of the garden, at ten in the morning it was not open. A few yards from where she stood was the door in the wall through which the mysterious Antoine Robelin had walked to his death. Flanking the doorway was one of Miss Jekyll's favourite "garden pictures", consisting of *Yucca gloriosa* in a massive clump, flanked by *Euphorbia wulfenii** and livened up by red hot pokers to give colour. The gap between the yucca and the *Clematis montana* on the wall behind it made an admirable hiding place. One could imagine Robelin strolling through the door and the assassin leaping out of Miss Jekyll's garden picture to knife him.

Except that the door was normally kept locked. Who had opened it? How? Why? Was there an alternative route round the end of the enclosing wall, outflanking it? No, unless one forced a passage in an armoured car. Nothing less would penetrate the main obstacle, an ancient rambler rose covered with thorns and small red hips. It was the size of a haystack and

*"One of the grandest and most pictorial of plants of recent acquirement for garden use." (G.J.) But its claims to nobility have now been challenged by the pundits, who say that it is not entitled to a specific name of its own, but is a mere sub-species of *E. characias*.

looked as if it knew exactly where to find an intruder's jugular vein.

"Good morning. You should have seen it in June," said a voice behind her. The door in the wall was open. Julian had just come through it.

"It was a fountain of blossom then," said Mary as she followed him through the doorway. "You recognize it?"

"Is it 'The Garland'?" Celia asked.

"That's right, it was her favourite rose,* she let them ramp everywhere, just cutting out the old wood every few years."

Celia had to remind herself that this conversation was taking place on the site of a recent, rather messy murder. It was typical of the Lindsays' attitude to disaster. On the Day of Judgment they would keep up a valiant flow of small talk and pretend that nothing untoward was happening.

"I'm sorry to have to inflict this boring meeting on you," said Julian. "We have to have them under the Trustees Act, but it won't take long. Do come in."

Celia had been looking forward to this. A house by Gertrude's architect friend Edwin Lutyens was always exciting to explore. In a typical Lutyens device to underline the surprise of the airy spaces within, the entrance porch was low and deeply shadowed by an overhanging roof. Mary Lindsay walked into its darkness from the brilliant sunshine, then halted and bent double with a gulping screech of disgust. "Oh how filthy, Julian, how dare they, I shall vomit."

It was the scene in the Lily Court over again, with Mary screaming hysterically and Julian shouting at her to control herself and dragging her away. By the time Celia's dazzled eyes had adjusted enough for her to see into the shadows, Adam had come running across the drive into the porch. "She's screaming again, what's happened now?"

Celia pointed to the dead cat strung up by its feet from the light fitting. "It hit her in the face as she walked in from the sunlight."

*Miss Jekyll urged her readers to get up at 4 a.m. in mid-June to admire its newly opened buds.

61

Muttering something, Adam brushed past her and went to intervene between his parents, whose quarrel echoed from somewhere upstairs. Left alone, Celia decided she might as well employ herself usefully. Having found the kitchen and collected a knife from it, she cut down the dead cat and deposited it in the dustbin in the back yard. The row upstairs was still going on, so she settled down to await events in a vast living-room of dramatic Lutyens proportions, with muted colours setting off the natural wood of the joinery. No wonder the Lindsays clung to their house, despite the hellish problems raised by its garden.

A car could be heard arriving. Footsteps clattered down the stairs. Julian, very red in the face, ushered in Barbara Seymour.

"What's been going on?" she asked.

"Nothing," said Julian loudly. "Mary will be down in a moment, Adam's with her."

Silence fell. It was not clear whether the dead cat had to be kept secret from Barbara, or whether it could not be discussed with Barbara in front of Celia.

Presently Mary appeared, escorted by Adam and making an enormous effort to seem normal. Julian had circulated papers for the meeting in advance. He called it to order round a table in one of the deep window recesses and began guiding it through the agenda with smooth Civil Service expertise. Of the others Barbara Seymour seemed out to prove that she was just as good at committee work as Julian and far better than anyone else, slapping Celia down when she asked sensible and relevant questions. Adam leapt to Celia's defence several times, and was gentle with Mary, whose contribution consisted of irrational gut reactions and protests against any proposal for change. His behaviour confirmed that he was at daggers drawn with his father, and he was sharp with Barbara, taking every chance to expose her ignorance of horticulture. It was clear that he resented her presence on the board and his doodle, which he did not attempt to hide, was a savage caricature of a finger-wagging Barbara laying down the law.

Most of the questions to be decided were about money. It seemed to Celia that the investment portfolio behind the trust was alarmingly small, the whole enterprise depended in a hand-to-mouth manner on the entrance fees, and even so there was a biggish deficit. By reassembling figures which Julian had carefully distributed between different pieces of paper, she worked out that he was subsidizing the garden to the tune of about £9,000 a year from his salary. If he had to find sums of this order, no wonder he had taken a well paid private sector job instead of retiring on his comfortable Civil Service pension.

When repair work to be done during the winter had been discussed and estimates approved for redecorating the tea-barn, Julian looked round enquiringly. "Any other business?"

Celia hesitated. Julian and Barbara had obviously written her off as a harmless little goose, and although she longed to break the taboo and insist on discussing dead cats and vandalized flower beds, it seemed a pity to blow this useful cover. In view of the Lindsays' ostrich-like attitude to disasters, to introduce Robelin's corpse into Any Other Business would have been even more unthinkable. She kept quiet, but longed to know if the police were any nearer finding out how on earth he fitted in.

She was glad she had not asked, because Julian himself brought up the subject over coffee after the meeting broke up. "The police have one hopeful lead," he reported. "They think it significant that Robelin's home village is only a few miles from Bruay-en-Artois." He paused. "I confess that the name meant nothing to me till they reminded me, but Bruay was the scene of a murder some years ago that became a political *cause célèbre*, and they think there may be some connection with this man Robelin in the background of the case."

"Bruay-en-Artois! That's right," cried Celia before she could stop herself. "A sex murder, wasn't it?"

"How curious that you should remember," said Julian. Adam was looking at her oddly too.

Celia beat a hasty retreat. "I think I drove through there once and the name stuck in my mind, but I forget the details. Do remind me."

"It's a mining village, I imagine one of those ugly places you

63

find up near the Belgian border. Only miners lived there, apart from the village notary and a widow who owned some property and one or two others like that who kept themselves to themselves in a little middle-class clique. Then a woman was murdered and the background was obviously sexual, and the village made up its mind that someone in this small circle was guilty and the others were covering up for him."

"How long ago was this?" Celia interrupted.

"I'm not sure, they didn't say. The political scandal developed because the examining magistrate investigating the case was very left wing. He decided for no obvious reason that the working class gossips were right, and turned the investigation into a blatant anti-bourgeois witch hunt. He kept telling the press he knew someone in the village upper-crust was guilty, but he couldn't produce any solid evidence and in the end he behaved so provocatively that he was taken off the case. That blew the thing up into a nationwide ding-dong battle between right and left, and it even made the British press. The left claimed that the politicians had interfered with the judiciary to protect a guilty member of the bourgeoisie, and the right replied that examining magistrates were supposed to collect evidence instead of airing their ideological prejudices."

"Was anyone ever found guilty?" Celia asked.

"No. And an unsolved murder rankles for years in a small community like that."

Celia knew she was asking too many questions, but could not resist it. "Why do they think this could be the background to the Robelin killing?"

"Some long-term revenge, perhaps. He was a notary, and he lived quite near Bruay."

Celia was disconcerted. She had been taking it for granted that Robelin was connected somehow with the central mystery of Monk's Mead. As far as she could remember the Bruay-en-Artois business had happened ten or fifteen years ago. Did the police really think Robelin had fallen victim to an ancient French curse?

When she left, Adam followed her out to her car. "Nearly

64

gave yourself away then, didn't you?" he said with a quick, taut smile.

"I . . . don't quite understand."

"Too well up in famous murders. The name Bruay-en-Artois clicked at once. Has it all started to make sense?"

"I'm sorry, I still don't know what you're hinting at."

He looked round the entrance court nervously. "We can't talk here. And, oh dear, we're open to the public soon. Would you mind awfully driving your car round to the public car park and letting yourself in that way — Julian did give you a key? And come to my house, we can talk there."

"Is that the cottage at the end of the pergola? Where Tessa and her young man were besieged by your parents?"

"That's right, she's living with me for the summer. Do come, we really must talk."

"Very well, but what is to be the subject of our conversation?"

A mischievous twinkle crossed his hawk-like face. "I know a bit more about you than you think, Mrs Grant. The others don't. You see, my ex-wife's sister works at Melsingham, she's the duchess's secretary."

"That nice Miss Moffat? Oh, I see."

"Yes, so I know all about the old lady who forged the pictures, and the business in New Zealand.* That was why I persuaded Graham Harrison to get you on the board, so that you could make sense of what's going on here."

Fine, but how the hell do I do that, Celia thought in dismay. He turned to go and she made for her car, which was parked next to Barbara Seymour's.

"Oh! One moment, Mr Lindsay, can you make sense of this for a start?"

"What? Do call me Adam, by the way."

"Thank you. A very dead bird is occupying the driving seat of Miss Seymour's car. A crow. Rather maggotty."

"Dear me yes, very gruesome, I'll get a spade and bury it." The taut grin reappeared on his face. "I'd leave it there as a

*See *Green Trigger Fingers* and *A Botanist at Bay* by the same author.

65

nasty surprise for Barbara, but I can't risk another shock for Mother."

Celia was astonished. Did he really hate Barbara so much that he could take this sickening sight in his stride? Surely he could see that it was the work of someone very nasty as well as very mad?

"George? We got something new on that kitchen knife. A Mrs Murphy that works part time in the Monk's Mead tea-barn remembers when it went missing."

"We know that already, it was on the morning of the murder."

"But this Mrs Murphy says she was cutting a cake into portions with it and turned her back for a moment and it was gone. She thought one of the others had taken it and went to get another."

"Yes, well?"

"She was cutting up her damn cake on the counter. The place was open to the public. Anyone could have picked it up. A customer, not just one of the staff who had access to the kitchen."

"Do you understand what's going on?" Celia asked as she sipped Adam's inferior sherry.

"No." Suddenly he looked defenceless. A hawk, but moulting.

"Does Graham Harrison know?"

"Probably, but he won't talk. Did you try?"

"Yes. The same thing. And now he's gone on holiday."

Adam nodded. "I think he saw the crisis coming. That's why he wanted to get out from under and put you in instead."

"Did he know you'd cast me as the Mata Hari of Monk's Mead?"

"No. No one knows except me."

They were sitting in the kitchen of the cottage. With his wife gone the house had a comfortless feel, the kitchen seemed to be the only downstairs room in use. There were tubes of paint and a palette on the dresser and an unfinished oil sketch of magnolias propped against the wall.

"You might have warned me of your far from honourable

66

intentions," said Celia.

"I was afraid of frightening you off. You told Harrison you were too busy to be a trustee."

"Worse and worse, your pretences are as false as mine."

"Yours are marvellous, they've decided you're as harmless as you look. If you'd rushed in with a lot of questions and put them on their guard, you'd have been treated to boiling oil from behind a defensive wall of misinformation."

"What's behind the defensive wall?" Celia asked.

"The fact that the aggro started before my grandmother died of her overdose. It was nothing to do with religious maniacs disapproving of euthanasia."

"Quite. She died *after* the gardeners left in a body and were replaced by the present ones. And now there seems to be a ground rule that the new ones mustn't be suspected of vandalizing the garden."

Adam produced his taut grin of excitement. "Exactly. If Dad admits that it's possible to suspect them, he admits that the aggro started before the official starting date."

"Your grandmother also died *after* your father was beaten up in London, but I suppose that could be a coincidence."

"Except that he was beaten up twice, with a week's gap between. That doesn't look like a coincidence."

"Twice? Are you sure?"

"Yes. The first time he told Mother he'd fallen downstairs at the flat. He struggled up to London to work as usual the week after, but she was worried about him, so I made an excuse and went up to the chrysanthemum show at the RHS and looked in on him in the evening. Since I'd seen him he'd acquired a lot of extra bruises and some broken ribs, and the flat had been more or less wrecked. What puzzled me at the time was, he pretended he'd only been beaten up once."

"Once could be passed off as a coincidence, twice couldn't. Same problem as the gardeners having to be above suspicion."

"Not just above suspicion," Adam corrected. "They mustn't be sacked when they're caught red-handed."

"You mean, that happened?"

67

"Yes, I was amazed. I caught one of them at it, a man called Martin Blake, and reported him to Dad. Dad hummed and hawed and said he'd deal with it. That was on a Wednesday, a few days before Uncle Anthony's statue came in for attention. Blake disappeared from view and I understood he'd been sacked, but by the middle of the week he was back on the job."

"Did your father explain at all?"

"According to Dad, George the head gardener complained of being short-handed and there wasn't anyone else. Also, Blake had threatened us with a fuss from his union about wrongful dismissal, and that would mean publicity about the vandalism, which Mother was dead keen to avoid. Anyway, Dad said the evidence wasn't cast iron."

"Wasn't it?"

"It was good enough for me. I found Blake in the Orange Garden one evening, long after he should have knocked off. He couldn't explain what he was doing there, and afterwards I found a sprayer full of Tumbleweed hidden in one of the borders. Dad said there was no evidence that Blake was responsible for putting it there. He also said that all the gardeners had alibis for the day the magnolia was cut down, therefore none of them was a vandal."

"How naive of him, alibis are not always what they seem."

"Actually, he cut it down himself, before we went out for the day. To 'prove' that the vandal wasn't a gardener."

"Dear me, not naive at all. Are you sure?"

"Yes, when we got back that night he suggested a stroll in the garden so that he could be prostrated with horror on 'discovering' the damage to the magnolia, and assure us that it had been perfectly all right when he 'happened' to take an early morning stroll through the Wild Garden before we left on our expedition. He was like some third-rate repertory actor in an old-fashioned melodrama, I was very embarrassed."

"Adam, at what stage in life's journey did you decide that your father had horns and a tail?"

"Ages ago, I've always hated the way he bullies Mother. Look how he's making her feel guilty now. That whole

68

performance was for her benefit, he cut down a marvellous and very rare tree to make sure she didn't put two and two together about the gardeners and realize that the aggro wasn't her fault, it was nothing to do with what happened over Gran's pills."

There was a silence. Adam was looking at her with a haunted expression as he waited for the next question.

"What did happen over the pills?" said Celia, asking it.

"This is the bit that gives me nightmares. I think Mother must have done it."

"Not him?"

"No. He was in London."

"Barbara, then?"

"Why would she?"

"She seems to have a special relationship with your father. They were contemporaries at Cambridge."

"She claims to have been at an educational conference in Brighton."

"Well, you know my opinion of alibis. If theirs are sound we have to fall back on a mercy killing by a devoted daughter, because Mrs Mortlock was in great pain."

"She'd been in pain for years, it was controllable to some extent with drugs. There must have been an extra motive to make Mother do it."

"What sort of motive?"

He thought for a moment. "I can imagine her killing her mother to spare her the distress of knowing something that she'd have had to know if she'd lived. I think she killed Gran to save her from knowing whatever's behind the aggro against Dad."

"Aren't we assuming that your mother doesn't know about that?" Celia objected.

"I think she wonders about a lot of things and then shuts her eyes to them."

"You haven't discussed all this with her?"

"I tried to, but we're the sort of family that doesn't discuss things that matter. When I tried to make her talk about it she got quite hysterical and locked herself in her room."

69

This seemed to Celia rather feeble of him. "You're much closer to her than you are to your father. Can't you have another go?"

He poured out more sherry, spilling some on the kitchen table. "You don't realize how difficult communications are in our family. Not just Dad, there's a wall between me and her too. One can't say to one's mother 'How on earth can you put up with the disgusting man who purports to be my father?'."

"Purports? I don't understand."

He rose and stared out of the window. "They're not my real parents. I think the communication difficulties started when I discovered that."

"Then . . . you're adopted?"

"That's right, finding out was a tremendous shock. A boy at school repeated something he'd overheard his father say, and of course I had to get to the bottom of it."

"D'you know who your natural parents are?"

"My unnatural parents refused to tell me, but I've always assumed that I'm a by-blow of Uncle Anthony's, in which case it follows that Barbara Seymour is my mother."

"I'm sorry," said Celia, thunderstruck, "but the logic of that escapes me."

"Oh, didn't you know? This bit is public property, more or less. She's the 'beloved' he wrote all those poems to."

"But Adam, how astonishing." It was impossible to imagine the formidable Barbara involved in procedures necessary for the production of a child.

"I know, but it must be right, the dates fit. The bit she wrote for the Memoir makes it fairly clear that she 'gave herself' to him on the eve of battle like a true Englishwoman, regardless of the consequences. That happened in Blackpool a month before he was killed and the consequences, exactly nine months later, were me."

"Is this more or less acknowledged in the family?"

"Absolutely not. I asked her once if she was my mother and she went puce with rage and respectability and reported me to Dad, who upbraided me for impertinence and attacked me savagely on the bottom with a walking stick."

"Is this the reason why scholarly research into Anthony Mortlock is embargoed?"

"I suppose so, but why are they so violent about it? When Tessa brought Peter Barton to see them with a list of questions, Mother had a sort of fit and Dad behaved like the smooth chucker-out at an expensive gambling joint. Tessa was furious, and she took it out on me."

"How unfair, it wasn't your fault."

"No, but there was a stand-up row and I didn't support her, how could I? I have to live and work here, taking sides would have made my position impossible. She wanted young Barton to be shown all the dirty linen, and anyone who tried to hide it was a filthy fascist."

"But Adam, what does the dirty linen consist of? Are you sure Barbara Seymour's your mother? Why is she called 'K——' and not 'B——' in the Memoir?"

"Because, believe it or not, Uncle Anthony used to call her 'Kitten'."

Suddenly they were both roaring with laughter. It was a relief, the last few minutes had been rather tense.

"You mean, the poems are headed 'To Kitten, on our Anniversary' and so on?" Celia asked.

"I think he usually wrote 'Kit' on the manuscript. Less embarrassing."

Having inadvertently produced a child, how would Barbara be expected to treat it? Like the kind of spider which eats its young? Or would she rear it as a single parent in an aura of social responsibility and government blue books? Neither, in the moral climate of 1942. "Has she always taken an interest in you?" she asked.

"Oh dear me yes, that's been one of the troubles. Mother and Gran loathed her but she kept pushing her way in here and Dad encouraged her. She's always taken a rather bossy interest in me, as if she owned me, I suppose that's why she came. When I left school she more or less ordered me to go to a university, and when I said 'no, I want to go to an art school' she was disgusted with me and said that wasn't a proper intellectual discipline and how dare I have no ambition and no brains. I've taken a lot of flak from her over the years, and as you've probably gathered, we're barely on speaking terms. Till I cured her of the habit by being stinkingly rude, she used to get me into a corner every six months or so and say gardening was no occupation for a man, and why the hell didn't I cut loose and go to an art school if that was what I wanted to do."

"Forgive me, but why didn't you?"

"How could I leave Mother in the lurch? Her husband was a pain in the neck, the garden was all she'd got, it was and is her whole life. She couldn't manage without me, I have to help if she's to keep it going. Anyway, I was never given a choice. When they'd put me through horticultural college I was simply told that I was coming back here to help Mother with the garden while Dad earned enough to subsidize it when it made a loss, and wasn't I lucky, because one day I'd inherit Monk's Mead and have the privilege and duty of handing it on intact to future generations."

"Am I right in thinking that this prospect horrifies you?"

He frowned. "Let me ask you a question. Why are the blown-up photos in the tea-barn all of Gertrude Jekyll's own garden at Munstead Wood, not of this one as it was in her day?"

"I assume, because no one took photographs of this one."

"There's a full set, they used to hang in the barn. We took them down fifteen years ago. Even then the garden had become unrecognizable, the plantings had got shapeless because trees and shrubs had grown enormous or died. A lot of the standard Jekyll herbaceous things had become too inbred or disease-prone to use. If we'd left the pictures up, the customers would have seen that our authentic Gertrude Jekyll garden was a travesty of the one she created. It's a farce, one day it will have to stop."

"Sir Julian told me in a very emphatic voice that there are legal reasons why you have to slog on regardless," said Celia, "but there's nothing about that in the trust deed."

"No, that's another mystery. There was a frightful family

row when the trust was being set up, I can just remember being terrified by it, I was five. There's another document somewhere, I believe, signed by my grandmother at the same time as the trust deed, that says what's to happen if the trust fails."

"You don't know what's in it?" Celia asked.

"It's about what happens to the money, I suppose."

"That's not a 'legal reason'. Besides, what's in the kitty isn't really worth bothering about. I think the old lady's blackmailing him from beyond the grave. If he stops subsidizing the garden, the lawyers produce a document containing something very embarrassing that he doesn't want known."

Adam's taut grin of excitement reappeared. "What a fascinating idea," he said and fell silent, enjoying it.

Celia fell silent too. They are all paralysed, it's a deadlock, she thought. Mary inherited the duty to preserve a labour-intensive garden which is hardly worth preserving in its present form. Julian has to go on subsidizing it because of whatever hold the old lady had over him. Adam is chained to Monk's Mead by his attitude to Mary with its strident Oedipal overtones. "That garden is a trap," she said aloud.

"I know. My wife, bless her, is the only one who got away. She said we must both escape from Monk's Mead before it crippled our lives. I couldn't leave Mother in the lurch, so we split up. Tessa's on my wife's side really, I thought I might get nearer her if I had her here for the summer, but we're both getting uptight, it's not working out."

"I'm sorry," said Celia and meant it.

He grinned again. "It's ironic really. Gertrude had to give up painting and take to gardening because her eyesight got bad, and I'm chained to the garden she created although I've always wanted to be a painter." He reached across the table and clutched her arm. "Monk's Mead isn't viable any more, even Mother's getting no satisfaction from it. I want you to stir things up, shatter the mould. That's why I got Graham Harrison to bring you in as a trustee."

Celia was about to protest against this alarming extension of her responsibilities when the door crashed open and Tessa

73

stormed in, dark-eyed and tense like her father.

"Hullo Pop, guess what Sir Julian and Lady Senile Dementia have done now," she began in a fury. "They've — oh." Seeing Celia, she broke off.

Celia made a polite pretence of preparing to leave.

"No, stay, you'd better hear this," said Adam. "What's happened, Tessa?"

"They've kidnapped Peter Barton and stolen all the dirt about Superpoet from his desk."

"Oh no, really!"

"Oh yes Pop really, get your head up out of the pretty flowers and take a look at the jungle law of the animal kingdom. They've kidnapped Peter, why? Because Superpoet has to stay lily white, we must all agree that he never said a cross word to anyone and ·he never had acne and his sexual organs were purely ornamental, and anyone who says different is going to be shot and have his filthy scribblings burnt."

"Hey, hey, calm down," Adam protested. "What makes you think Barton's been kidnapped?"

"I had a date with Peter on Thursday and he didn't turn up and he didn't phone so in the end I rang him, and one of his flatmates answered. Peter hasn't been there for three days and his room's been burgled, someone broke his desk open and all his notes for his thesis have disappeared."

She turned to go.

"Wait," said Adam. "Where are you off to?"

"Up to the house to tell those two geriatric lunatics exactly what I think of them."

"Now just a minute, Tessa — " Adam began.

"There you go again, taking their side against me," Tessa stormed. In seconds, they were both shouting. The slanging match ranged over what seemed to be well-trodden ground without reaching a conclusion, and presently Celia ventured to interrupt. "May I ask you something, Tessa?"

"Who are you, anyway?"

"Mrs Grant," Adam explained, "is helping me try to discover what all this mystery is about. Your grandparents

74

don't know that, and you're not to tell them."

Tessa threw him a sudden smile. "Well done Pop, action at last, but Mrs Grant needn't bother. I'm going up to the house now to raise hysterical adolescent hell till they tell me what they've done with Peter."

"Whoa, whoa," said Celia. "Before you accuse them of kidnapping him, you ought to make quite sure of your ground. What exactly is missing from his desk? Did he say anything about where he was going before he disappeared? Do his relatives know where he is? Until you know everything there is to know you'll be in a weak position, your grandparents will have no trouble at all slapping you down."

Tessa looked sulky. "Then what d'you think I should do?"

"Go to his flat. Your grandmother may have dropped an incriminating ear-ring there for you to find."

To Celia's relief, Tessa giggled. "Creeping Christians, I believe you're right. Pop, be an angel, drive me to the station."

"But wait a minute," said Celia. "Have you a key to this flat?"

"No, my relations with Peter are too formal for that."

"Do all his flatmates work? If so, there's no point in going there till one of them gets home, unless you're prepared for a long wait on the doorstep."

A look of sulky frustration appeared on Tessa's face. From experience of her own children's teenage years, Celia knew at once what it signalled; the collapse of fragile self-confidence and a longing to be told firmly by an adult what to do.

"Look Tessa, why don't you work your shift in the tea-barn this afternoon, and I'll pick you up at five and — where is this flat?"

"West Kensington."

"Fine, I'll drive you there and we'll see what we can find out."

"Oh. Would you really? Thank you."

"That's all right, I have to be in London tomorrow to judge late-flowering shrubs at the Horticultural Hall. I'll put you on the late train and spend the night at my club."

75

"May I speak to Sir Julian Lindsay, please?"

"I suppose so if you insist, but I told you not to phone me here."

"Ah, you recognize my voice. You told me a great many things, and I told you some too but, alas, it's what the French call a dialogue of the deaf, we don't listen to each other, do we? Hence the need for these unpleasant little surprises, to reinforce what one is trying to say."

"Littering my premises with decomposing animal corpses isn't getting you anywhere, I wish you'd stop it."

"Don't let's exaggerate, my dear fellow. I'm sure the wretched Robelin was removed before he had time to decompose, and aren't you missing the point? The game is called Animal, Vegetable and Mineral. The dead animals would not have been necessary if my little vegetable reminders in your garden had proved more effective, and of course the knife that killed Robelin was mineral. You brought the Robelin business on yourself, I did warn you."

"When you're arrested for that, you'd better plead diminished responsibility. I could give you the name of a very good man in Harley Street, but I'm afraid it's too late. You've been teetering on the verge of criminal lunacy for years, and now you're well over the edge."

"Oh dear, you are making me very, very angry."

"I daresay, and you're boring the pants off me. Don't ring me again for a bit, I'm supposed to be on holiday."

"Could we clear up one thing for a start," said Tessa as Celia drove her into London against the flow of the evening rush hour. "Peter isn't my boy friend, much too pompous. He's just a research student who's interested in Great-Uncle Anthony and wants to find out more about him. I said I'd help because I believe in people finding out what they want to know."

"D'you know how much he's found out already?" Celia asked.

"He says there are lots of poems people don't know about. My great-grandmother owned the copyright and wouldn't let them be published."

"Why? Weren't they good enough?"

"Peter says they're very good and throw quite a new light on Superpoet."

"He's seen them then?"

"Only three or four of them. Last autumn copies in Great-Uncle Anthony's handwriting came up for auction at Sotheby's. Peter went to the viewing day. He thinks there are a lot more like them that have been suppressed, all written after the great brainstorm when he left the Intelligence place in the country and joined the army. Peter calls them the "black" poems, they're full of the most marvellous indignation against the bunglers and crypto-fascists who let Hitler get away with it for so long and then made a mess of fighting the war."

"And Mrs Mortlock suppressed them because she thought them too anti-Establishment?"

"That's right. Peter wrote to her for copyright permission, so that he could publish the ones he'd seen at Sotheby's in his thesis and she said 'no'. Then when she died and Gran inherited the copyrights he thought he'd try again. I brought him here to talk to her and ask her a few questions about Great-Uncle Anthony, it was awful. Grandfather was there as well and they both barked at him like dogs guarding a bone, they couldn't have been nastier if he'd been a burglar or an anti-nuclear demonstrator. He tried to interview Barbara Seymour too, but they must have warned her. She was very calm and cold and said she'd nothing to add to what she'd written for the Memoir."

"Did Peter discover anything else about Mortlock, apart from the fact that he wrote the black poems?"

"I don't know," said Tessa. "He talked a lot about his thesis, but without saying much about what was in it. It seems to be a cut-throat world, they're all afraid someone else who's writing a thesis on the same subject will pinch bits of their research."

According to Tessa, his research had been thorough. Besides consulting documentary sources he had spent much time interviewing people who had known Mortlock. He had told Tessa pompously that some of the things he had been told posed "fundamental questions whose import I don't wholly understand". Recently there had been some kind of break-through, nature unspecified, which had excited him greatly and made everything clear. Since then he had been working flat out to get the thesis finished, because he was in a neck and neck race for priority with another thesis-writer on Mortlock, name not revealed to Tessa, who might have made some of the same discoveries. It occurred to Celia that Peter's supervisor in Cambridge would know what line of research he was following, but according to Tessa he was in the United States on holiday and unavailable.

Peter Barton's flat had been carved out of the top floor of a gaunt Victorian terrace house in West Kensington. It was inhabited not by a group of friends but by a collective of comparative strangers sharing out the rent. Two of his flat-mates were back from work, but seemed to know very little about him. After much discussion they established that he had last been seen there on the Thursday of the previous week, but they did not keep track of each others' comings and goings and had no reason to think his disappearance sinister. Had he really been kidnapped? Celia would have suspected not, but for the fact that his desk had been almost reduced to matchwood by someone determined to get at the contents of its locked drawers. Blank paper had been scattered about the room, but the intruder had left behind nothing written or typewritten. He had come up the fire escape and forced the bathroom window. Barton's was the only room he had touched.

"How did he know which was Peter's?" Tessa asked.

"Easy," said Celia. "Watch him for a day or two, take a note of his clothes, look in all the wardrobes in the flat till you see a garment you recognize." She reverted to the desk. "When did this happen?"

Again, the information was vague because it was not normal for the inhabitants to enter each others' rooms. The desk had been found wrecked on the previous day, when someone came in to leave a message on it for Barton. He seemed to be something of a joke to his flatmates. Keeping his desk locked was of a piece with solemn, methodical habits and he was pompous about his thesis, but without saying what was going to be in it. When not out of London to interview people who had known Anthony Mortlock, he worked in the British Museum reading room or the reference room at the London Library.

There were some letters addressed to Barton lying in the hall of the flat. Two were obvious circulars, a third looked like a bank statement. Celia began to tear open the remaining one.

"D'you think we should?" said Tessa.

"In the circumstances, yes." Celia broke off and began to search through the typewritten pages. It was the catalogue of a forthcoming Sotheby's sale of manuscripts and rare books. Lot 97 had been sidelined for Barton's attention: three unpublished autograph poems by Anthony Mortlock.

On the way downstairs Tessa said: "That was a fat lot of use. We still don't know where Peter is or why my hellish grandparents burgled his desk."

"Did they? Can you see either of them shinning up a fire escape and climbing through a smallish bathroom window into the flat?"

"Who else, then?"

"Who vandalized the garden at Monk's Mead? Who beat up your grandfather? Who murdered a Frenchman who was about to ring your grandparents' front door bell, and what did the Frenchman intend to say to them? How d'you know that the murderer isn't very interested indeed in the contents of Peter's desk?"

"You mean, my grandparents know something, and this other person knows it too, and they're having a private war with each other about it; some bit of dirt about Superpoet that they don't want published and he does."

"Not quite," said Celia. "If he knows it, why doesn't he go ahead and publish? I think he's keeping it secret too, so that he can use it somehow."

"This is all very well," said Tessa impatiently. "But Peter's got to be found, I'm not going back to Monk's Mead to sit on my bottom, we must do something."

Celia considered. Clearly this craving for action had to be satisfied. "Why don't you hang around here till his other flatmates come home, and see if they know anything about his movements? And you could get on to his parents, there must be some way of finding out their address, they may know something. I have various lines to follow up, I'm going to my club now to get on the phone. I'm busy tomorrow morning, but let's meet for lunch and compare notes. Where? Why not the porch of the National Gallery at one?"

So saying, Celia left her and checked in for the night at her club, where she grabbed at the telephone.

"May I speak to Colonel Fortescue? It's Celia Grant."

"Hold on, I'll see," said the woman he had married indecently soon after Celia, freshly widowed, had turned him down.

"Celia, how nice to hear from you," he said.

"Not really, Charles, I'm only ringing because I want something from you. D'you still work at the War Office?"

"Yes, except that nowadays we think it more tactful to call it the Ministry of Defence."

"Then could you find out from the records what Pilot Officer Anthony Mortlock was doing in 1940 and 1941? Some sort of Intelligence job."

"Mortlock? Isn't that the war poet?"

"Yes. Whatever he was doing was very hush-hush and high-level. But it must have stopped being hush-hush years ago, I'm sure you can find out."

"Only if I give a very good reason for looking him up in the files of a department that's nothing to do with me."

"Then will you please invent a reason? You know what would be appropriate, I don't."

"Anything to oblige, but Celia, what are you up to?"

"Nothing, the family want to know because they're commissioning a new biography," Celia lied. If she told him about the carry-on at Monk's Mead he would become masculine and protective and make a huge chivalrous fuss. This was largely why she had refused to marry him.

"Is that you, Bill? This is Annie."
"Who?"

80

"Oh how shaming, don't you remember me? From the tea-barn at Monk's Mead."

"Oh yeah. Hullo there, Annie."

"I've discovered something quite sensational that you ought to know."

"Have you, Annie? That's nice, what is it then?"

"I can't explain on the phone, I'd have to show you. How about a drink this evening at the Six Bells?"

"Listen Annie, it's kind of difficult. I can't, not tonight."

"Tomorrow night, then?"

"I'm sorry, I've a lot on just now. How about I ring you one day next week when I know how I'm fixed?"

"Not till then? Don't you want a scoop?"

"Sorry love. How did you find out my phone number?"

"It was written in quite large letters on the side of the van you gave me a lift in. 'Bye for now."

Celia spent a busy morning at the Horticultural Hall serving on Floral Committee B, which in its collective wisdom awarded a preliminary commendation to a new hypericum cultivar and refused one to an allegedly new eucryphia, which it denounced as having been brought to the Society's notice in 1934 as a sport of *E.nymanensis*. Shortly before one she was climbing the steps of the National Gallery, high above the swirling traffic in Trafalgar Square. Tessa was there already, looking tense and bursting with bad news, but Celia settled her down with wine and sandwiches in a pub in St Martin's Lane before she would let her begin.

"It's very frightening, Celia. Peter's parents are on holiday abroad, so I can't find out anything from them, and Peter hasn't been seen at the flat since last Thursday. There's a girl lives there, she came in soon after you left. Peter's keen on her but she doesn't go for him. He told her on the Wednesday evening that he had to go down to Sunningdale in the morning."

"Why Sunningdale? Did he say?"

"Yes, he was a bit annoyed about that. He'd finished the research, he was writing it up flat out to get it in before the other thesis someone's writing about Great-Uncle Anthony. And then someone rang to say they'd heard he was interested in Anthony Mortlock, and they had some unpublished manuscript poems of his, and would Peter come down to Sunningdale to look at them. Peter had to go, because apparently if you're writing a thesis everything has to go in, the assessors treat you as a criminal if you leave a known fact out."

Sunningdale, Celia thought grimly. A scattered community of big houses in their own grounds, inhabited by the sort of people who could afford that kind of house; among them pop stars, stockbrokers, industrialists, rich Arabs, probably one or two people whose sources of wealth were best not enquired into. A place where everyone minded his own business and no one knew what went on behind next door's shelter belt of *Rhododendron ponticum.*

Somewhere in Sunningdale lived one of the people who had known Anthony Mortlock; someone who had been interviewed about him by Peter Barton and had taken alarm because the questions revealed that Barton knew far too much.

So the trap had been baited with "unpublished Mortlock manuscripts" and set. And Barton had walked straight into it.

FIVE

"*Hullo Kitty dear, how are you on this lovely hot August morning?*"

"*You must have the wrong number. There's no one called Kitty here.*"

"*Oh but there is Kitty dear, I recognized your dulcet tones at once. How dreadful, you're living in a fantasy world, pretending you're not called Kitty and don't have a scarlet past. That sort of thing spells havoc for your mental health.*"

"*Now look here —*"

"*Don't interrupt, it's rude. And don't hang up on me like you did before, or I'll be very, very cross, and you know what that leads to.*"

"*I'm very cross already. What d'you want now?*"

"*Oh what a naughty bad-tempered voice, you ungrateful thing. I rang to talk to you for your own good, did Sotheby's send you the catalogue?*"

"*Yes. This time I'm not going to bid.*"

"*Oh dear, how very unwise. Not bid for that embarrassing sonnet? Or that telltale little poem about you and the coffin? Both of them in that very distinctive handwriting?*"

"*I thought this time I'd let you buy them in.*"

"*But Kitty, I shan't buy them in, they'll go to some half-baked American university where an eager-beaver little researcher who's mad to publish something and get tenure will put all your youthful indiscretions into his thesis, surely you don't want that?*"

"*Of course not, nor do you but it's your problem. You put them up for sale.*"

"*I set the problems, you solve them.*"

"*Not this one. I'm not playing this game any more, you bid me up too high last time.*"

"*I had very heavy expenses to cover just then, I needed the money. Listen, this time I won't be greedy, I'll stop bidding you up at a thousand.*"

83

"They'll go for more than that to some dealer who remembers what the last lot fetched and hopes to sell in America at a profit."

"Then you'll have to outbid the dealer, won't you?"

"No, you'll have to buy them in."

"I wish I could, but I'm still having a cash flow problem which I'm afraid you'll have to solve."

"You've had all you're going to get out of me."

"Oh no, Kitty. I've only just begun."

Celia had a bad conscience as she watched Tessa vanish eagerly into the crowd, bound for Waterloo Station and Sunningdale. She was an admirable young person, impatient at secrecies and shams and conscientious in her determination to do the right thing by a pompous young man in whom she had no sentimental interest. Most of her political opinions were ludicrous, but in Celia's view there was something wrong with any student who was not infected for a time with the left-wing bug.

Celia had warned her what would happen when she told her story at Sunningdale police station. She would be treated as a hysterical female raising a kidnapping scare on insufficient evidence, probably after a lover's tiff. But Tessa, one had to respect her for it, was determined to go.

I should have gone with her, Celia thought, to back her up. But the same thing had happened to her once when she stumbled on a crime, she had been held up to ridicule as a mad busybody and waster of police time. In the end she had been proved right, but the experience had left its mark. She had let Tessa go alone out of cowardice, it was no use pretending otherwise.

But there were clues to be followed up in London, at Sotheby's for instance, where manuscripts of three Mortlock poems were on display before being auctioned. At the main auction rooms in Bond Street she was directed to an annexe, situated in the sort of narrow alley that prudent people avoid at night. It seemed hardly the place for selling rare books and manuscripts, but she persevered. Sure enough, a door bearing

84

the firm's august name led surprisingly into a discreetly lit hall with a decor which combined subtle suggestions of expense, modernity, tradition and expertise.

The manuscripts and books to be sold next day were on view in a small auction room opening off the hall. Armed with Peter Barton's catalogue, Celia soon identified Lot 97. The three poems, fair copied in a florid but legible hand, were on separate pages of yellowing paper which looked as if they had been torn out of the same notebook. In accordance with Mortlock's usual practice, all three were dated at the bottom of the page. She studied first a rollicking but very sour ballad dated April 10th 1942:

A SONG FOR THE GREY MEN

Hats off to the Obscenotaph
The phallic symbol which
When worshipped like the Golden Calf
Lands nations in the ditch.

Our empire is unsinkable
And we were born to reign,
But warfare was unthinkable
(We'd nothing much to gain).

Faced with the Hitler terror
We didn't flinch a bit.
We hoped he'd see his error,
So we appeased the shit.

Hurrah! For we the shirkers
Need no more glorious dead.
The peasants and the workers
Can die for us instead.

We are a noble nation.
England's a blessed plot.
Let's fight in moderation,
And fornicate a lot.

What was Celia to make of this, and how did the Cenotaph, erected to commemorate the dead of the First World War, fit in? She remembered riding up Whitehall on a bus as a small child with her grandfather, who took off his hat out of respect for the dead as they passed it. In the days when men wore hats that was probably quite common, but what had the Cenotaph to do with sex? Make love, not war? No, the reverse, it seemed. Make less love and more energetic war.

The date gave one a clue. In April 1942 Hitler's armies were striking deep into Russia, and the left in Britain was clamouring for a second front in Western Europe to relieve the pressure on Stalin. Perhaps this was where the Cenotaph fitted in. Roger, her husband, had always said that the memory of 1914–18 with its massive sacrifice of British lives, had dominated strategic thinking about the second front: an unsuccessful invasion of Europe involving heavy British casualties would be politically unacceptable as well as militarily disastrous, because of the memories it would revive of lives wasted by incompetent generals in World War One.

Clearly Mortlock did not accept this line of reasoning. According to him the "grey men" of the Establishment, having failed to stop Hitler in his tracks before the war started, were failing now to prosecute it vigorously enough. In that case the references to sex must be allegorical, symbolizing the decadent activities the "grey men" indulged in instead of doing their duty and coming to the rescue of beleaguered Russia.

The next poem was dated earlier: 15th December 1941. It contained an even more puritanical rejection of sex, but in a personal context:

TO KIT FOR CHRISTMAS

Why are you so grave and cold?
With blank eye sockets and no-nose nostrils
And that grin?

Why do you stand there beckoning like a harlot,
Cocking your pelvic bone and xylophonic rib-cage
And hank of hair?

86

Why trouble me? The spring was long ago.
You blow in vain upon dead embers
With winter's breath.

Get back in your coffin and lie down.
Someone is sure to jump in too and rape you
To your heart's content.

To a person of Celia's practical turn of mind these lines posed various non-literary questions. What had happened to transform "Kit", *alias* Barbara Seymour, from the beloved of the Collected Poems into a skeletal figure arousing violent distaste, then back again into the beloved whose passionate reunion with Mortlock in Blackpool had launched Adam Lindsay on life's journey? She was reading the poem again when a voice hissed in her ear: "Filthy sexist."

She turned. A red-haired young woman with glasses and a receding chin stood beside her, trembling with indignation as she gaped at the sepulchral poem. Assuming that the reproach was addressed to Mortlock rather than herself, she replied: "Yes, it is very nasty. But one doesn't know what she'd done to upset him."

"Does it matter?"

"It obviously did to him," said Celia.

"A poem should be read for its intrinsic message, don't you think, without taking irrelevant factors into account. Besides, isn't the situation perfectly clear? She got ill and he got tired of her. She pleaded with him not to abandon her, he turned a deaf ear and she died of neglect. And now he's projecting his guilt on to her by calling her a harlot."

"I see. Are you writing a thesis about Mortlock's work?"

"Yes: 'Sexism in World War Two poetry, with special reference to Anthony Mortlock'."

"But you won't be able to quote these poems, because the family won't give permission."

"I can refer to them, and say that they can't be quoted for copyright reasons. They're essential to my proof of the sexist sources of war. There was an even more explicit one in a batch of manuscripts that turned up at a sale here six months ago. It was about two lovers, and the weight of the man on the woman's body was quite obviously a symbol of politico-military as well as sexual oppression. Mortlock's a seminal figure for that period, there's enormous interest in him. That last batch of manuscripts fetched almost fifteen hundred pounds."

"I wonder if you've come across a young man called Peter Barton," Celia asked, "who is also researching into Mortlock?"

"Of course. Poor young man, he's obsessed with irrelevant biographical detail, the poetry goes straight over his head. I tease him from time to time, pretending I know a lot about Mortlock's life that he doesn't. You must excuse me now, I have to make copies of all these poems."

While she did so Celia studied the third poem, a sonnet with a date in September 1941:

"CLV"

From beauteous creatures we desire fair deeds,
Look in thy glass and see thy beauty's fate,
For inward treason like a canker feeds
On summer's buds and leaves them ruinate.
Dark as dread night can beauty's visage be;
Black is not foul unless its deeds be so.
Though thou art black, thy *will* had me in fee
Loving and loved, until love's overthrow.
Our joyful concord thou didst hold at naught
And with disdainful pride my trust betray.
To win another's favour, basely sought,
My gift, my tables thou didst gift away.
     When thou art old, by time's fell hand defac'd
     My rime shall haunt thee, till thou die disgrac'd.

"Good gracious, what on earth is this about?" Celia asked her rapidly scribbling neighbour.

The red-haired woman re-read the poem with pencil poised. "I should have thought that was obvious."

"Not to me. What sort of title is 'CLV'?"

"Shakespeare wrote a cycle of one hundred and fifty-four sonnets. Mortlock has added number one hundred and fifty-five, because he didn't think Shakespeare had been rude enough to the Dark Lady."

"Is it addressed to her?"

"Of course. 'Black' in Elizabethan English means dark-haired and dark-eyed."

Barbara Seymour's boot-button eyes were black. What colour had her hair been before it went white?

"But what does it mean? Who gifted away tables, and why?"

The red-haired woman studied the poem again. "I'm afraid you'll have to read my thesis to find out," she said and went on scribbling. Presently she snapped her notebook shut, ready to go.

"One moment. Do tell me your name?"

"I don't see what business that is of yours," said the young woman, and went.

Celia decided that she had better do some copying too. The sonnet in particular would have to be pored over for hours before it yielded its secret, for Shakespeare's sonnets were a gap in her education and her ideas about the Dark Lady were of the vaguest. As she set to work copying it into the blank pages at the back of her engagement diary, another Mortlock-fancier moved into position beside her. She glanced at her, saw who it was and moved away rapidly before she was recognized, then spied on her from behind her catalogue while pretending a deep interest in an autograph letter from Charles Dickens, asking his wine merchant to send round two bottles of port.

Barbara Seymour did not study the poems for long, but nodded at them crossly as if recognizing old acquaintances she was not pleased to see. After staring at them for a moment she turned abruptly away and strode past Celia towards the exit, with her face pinched into a look of concentrated fury.

"George? There's a telex in from Paris. That Bruay-en-Artois business is a dead duck, they say. The murder there happened nearly twenty years ago."

"Surprised, are you?"

"No. I always thought that, considering our source."

"Interesting, though. It confirms something we've always suspected about Sir Julian."

"Which would be fine, George, if we could make sense of what we suspect."

"We can, up to a point. He suggested Bruay-en-Artois to sell us the idea that Robelin was nothing to do with him or the garden. For the same reason, he's been spreading it around at Monk's Mead that Bruay-en-Artois is the police theory."

"We can't arrest him for that, but what the hell is his tie-up with Robelin?"

When Celia was sure that Barbara Seymour had gone for good, she finished making her copy of the three poems, then went to the desk and asked how much they were likely to fetch.

"It's hard to say, Madam. We had a rather larger batch of autograph poems by Anthony Mortlock in a sale six months ago. They fetched £1450."

"Which was a lot more than you expected?"

"We didn't know what to expect, Mortlock items don't often come up for sale. But there was, yes, a surprising amount of interest."

"General interest? Or just two people bidding each other up?"

"That's not a matter on which I'd care to comment."

Someone had clearly paid an inflated price, and that meant at least two rival bidders, perhaps more. Julian Lindsay? Barbara Seymour? The kidnapper of Peter Barton?

"I suppose you won't tell me who the successful bidder was?" she asked.

"I'm afraid not, but if you want to contact the purchaser, we would forward a letter."

Abandoning this line of enquiry, Celia decided that what she needed next was a library to clarify her mind about the Dark Lady, and that the one at the University of London would do. But an assistant librarian at the entrance queried her right of access to the riches of its towering Bloomsbury fortress, on the ground that she was not a member of the university.

"But I am," she decided on giving the matter thought. "I have a Master of Science degree in Horticulture from Wye Agricultural College in Kent, which is affiliated."

Having won her point, she was soon installed at a desk piled high with learned works on Shakespeare's sonnets, and was beginning to see why the English mistress at school had skated over them rather lightly. Generations of eminent scholars had twisted themselves into knots trying to escape from the shaming conclusion that England's national poet had addressed love poem after love poem to another man. "It may be asked," wrote a clergyman in 1870, "why such addresses were penned to one of his own sex. The judicious Shakespeare would never be guilty of such errors . . . ." The poems, he argued, were "satires" on the extravagant terms in which Elizabethan poets addressed their mistresses. Another writer maintained in 1916 that the person addressed was not a man, but "the personification of the poet's muse or genius. They should be read as the semi-conscious outpourings of the poetic imagination." A worried Indian Civil Servant had evolved a theory that five different writers, rivals in a poetry competition, had written sonnets addressed to no one in particular. As a second line of defence it was generally agreed that the addressee, if any, was not the obvious candidate but Lord Herbert, a child so young that the "love affair" had to be purely verbal.

There was also a good deal about the Dark Lady, who seemed to have involved herself in a confused triangular relationship with the two gentlemen. But apart from the fact that she both attracted and repelled Shakespeare, little seemed to be known about her. What exercised the pundits was that the sonnets about her introduced abrupt changes of subject within the cycle which interrupted its flow. Did this mean that they had been printed in the wrong order? Much scholarship was devoted to shunting the Dark Lady about in an attempt to accommodate her where she made sense.

Presently Celia discovered in her pile of books some more modern works which did not shrink from the implication that Shakespeare cherished warm feelings, whether consummated or not, for his first patron, the young Earl of Southampton. One writer even suggested that the Dark Lady did not exist, except as an allegorical figure representing the carnal as opposed to the sublime side of the Southampton-Shakespeare relationship. Celia read on, increasingly bewildered by the miscellaneous information she was collecting. Anything about a phoenix was a coded reference to homosexuality or alternatively to Queen Elizabeth the First, and to make matters more difficult the sonnets were full of coded references to phoenixes. The nursery rhyme "Cock-a-Doodle-Doo" was about castration and the word "will" was a euphemism for lust, or by transference the sexual organs. There was also some connection between the sonnets and Catharism, a convenient religious heresy combining strict puritanical ideals in theory with freedom in practice to do exactly as one liked.

Mortlock had accused his Dark Lady, presumably Barbara Seymour, of treacherously giving away "my gift, my tables". Scholars discussing Shakespeare's parallel passage made it clear that the "tables" were some form of notebook, possibly containing poems written by the donor, the Earl of Southampton. Apart from that they could add little to what Shakespeare himself had said about the episode:

CXXII

Thy gift, thy tables, are within my brain
Full character'd with lasting memory,
Which shall above that idle rank remain,
Beyond all date, even to eternity:
Or, at the least, so long as brain and heart
Have faculty by nature to subsist;
Till each to raz'd oblivion yield his part

Of thee, thy record never can be miss'd.
That poor retention could not so much hold,
Nor need I tallies thy dear love to score:
Therefore to give them from me I was bold,
To trust those tables that receive thee more:
  To keep an adjunct to remember thee
  Were to import forgetfulness in me.

Shakespeare, then, was excusing himself for having given away
Southampton's "tables", perhaps to the Dark Lady who had
then made mischief by sneaking on him to Southampton *via* the
third leg of the triangular relationship. In Mortlock's case the
situation was different. The "tables" belonged to him. He had
given them to Barbara Seymour and she had passed them on to
someone. Who? Julian Lindsay? He was the obvious candidate
and there was some tacit understanding between him and
Barbara Seymour. But the Shakespearean parallel must not be
pressed too far. There was no evidence that a love-triangle had
existed between the three of them, and even less reason to
suppose that one of its sides could have been a Mortlock-
Lindsay tie-up along the lines of the Southampton-Shakespeare
one. If Julian had been homosexual he would not have married
Mary while still in his twenties.

Determined to leave no stone unturned in her search for
truth, Celia had not limited her demands on the library to
books about Shakespeare. A check on a microfilm index had
revealed that two alumni of the university had produced theses
on Anthony Mortlock. Hoping that they had uncovered
answers to some of the questions about him, she had asked the
library to produce the fruits of their research. Presently, tiring
of Shakespearean erudition, she picked up the M.Litt. thesis on
Mortlock by one A. H. L. Harris, but found to her disgust that
he made no mention of the "black" poems. Mr Harris had
expended his energies on the innocuous ones passed for
publication by Mrs Mortlock, demonstrating laboriously that
they had been influenced hardly at all by Mortlock's World
War One predecessor, Rupert Brooke, though occasional

echoes of Swinburne, Kafka and Christina Rossetti were to be found as well as the dominating influence of Auden.

But where was the other thesis she had asked to see, the one by I. D. Cameron? The library was sorry, but she could not be shown it. Why not? Because there was a block on it. What did that mean? It meant that a thesis less than five years old could not be consulted without the writer's permission, and unfortunately I. D. Cameron's effort was almost six months too young.

"Then tell me how to get hold of him, and I'll ask for permission." said Celia.

But that was objected to as contrary to all the rules. The proper course was for the librarian to write to the author at the most recent address they had for him, and get in touch with Celia if and when they received a reply. Persuasion failed to get this inconvenient ruling reversed. But she decided not to give up, on the illogical principle that what she could not have must somehow be worth having. Since the writer of a D. Litt. thesis might well have gone on to an academic career, she consulted the Universities Year Book; searching first among Scottish universities in view of his name and rejecting Camerons who were engineers or had the wrong initials. A Dr I. D. Cameron who was a Senior Lecturer in Modern Literature at the University of Aberdeen seemed to be an odds-on favourite. Regardless of expense, she thrust a credit card into the first public telephone that would accept it, and rang Aberdeen. It was indeed the right Cameron and she explained her business.

"Ye may certainly see my thesis, Mrs Grant. But if it's what ye refer tae as the 'black' poems that interest ye, it'll not give ye much help. There's nae mention of them in it."

"I suppose the family refused permission to reproduce them?"

"I asked no permission. I didna know they existed until after my thesis had been finished and accepted."

"You mean, you only found out when the manuscripts started turning up at auction?"

"They have? I didna know that. Where?"

"At Sotheby's. There was a batch about six months ago, and

now the *Song for the Grey Men* and *To Kit for Christmas* and a very puzzling sonnet in imitation of Shakespeare."

"Ye have the advantage, these names mean nothing tae me. I never had sight of any of the poems he wrote after the so-called brainstorm."

"Then how did you know about them?"

Cameron explained that as part of the research for his thesis he had approached Andrew Stamford, the author of the Memoir, knowing that Stamford had been given access to family papers while preparing it. Stamford had made difficulties and excuses, but Cameron had kept pressing him till finally, when the draft thesis was almost complete, Stamford had agreed to see him. Even then he had parted with little or no information and Cameron had written him off as a very disagreeable old man.

"And then after my thesis had been accepted," he went on, "Stamford sent for me and told me about these terrible poems of depression that Mortlock wrote in the last year of his life."

All was explained. Stamford had acted as he did out of kindness. He knew a great deal that Mrs Mortlock had forbidden him to publish, and which could not be published as long as she kept her stranglehold on the copyrights. It would have been cruel to pass on to Cameron information that he could not use, but which would alter his whole view of the subject. The unfortunate Cameron would have had no choice but to abandon a thesis he had worked on for over a year.

"Is Stamford still alive?" Celia asked. "I can't find him in any of the reference books."

"He died two winters ago."

"Is there a widow? What happened to his literary papers?"

"If ye mean his papers about Anthony Mortlock, he had none."

This seemed hard to believe. Stamford must have announced in the literary press that he had been commissioned to write a biography. He would have asked anyone who had kept letters or papers connected with Anthony Mortlock to let him borrow and copy them. A biographer's dragnet of this kind often yielded information which came as a disagreeable surprise to the subject's family, and Stamford's haul probably contained most of the material that a shocked Mrs Mortlock had embargoed.

"I suppose the old lady made him hand everything over when he'd finished the Memoir," said Celia.

"She did not. By the time it was ready for publication the pair of them had fought like wildcats over every paragraph in it. The poor man yelled at her for making him violate his scholarly conscience and fudge over the truth, and she cursed him for trying tae slander her darling boy. She didna trust him tae hand over the papers he'd collected. She never even asked for them. She broke intae his house and stole them every one."

"Goodness. You're sure it was her?"

"She denied it and created a lot. But who else could it have been?"

This was a question that needed thinking about, but later. "Did Stamford tell you what caused the famous 'brainstorm of despair'?"

"He did not."

"But he must have known."

"He knew, but he considered himself bound by the Official Secrets Act."

"What nonsense, nothing's secret in this day and age about World War Two. Do I gather that it was connected with this Intelligence work of his?"

"That's so. All Stamford would tell me was, it was something tae do with his work at Bletchley Park."

"Was that where Mortlock was working?"

"So Stamford told me. Ye know what they were doing there at Bletchley?"

"Good Lord, yes. Is there anyone who doesn't?"

SIX

As Celia drove homeward out of London she tried to sort out the mass of undigested information in her head. Of the many unanswered questions the most puzzling seemed to be: who was the burglar who stole Andrew Stamford's hoard of Mortlock papers back in 1948? Mrs Mortlock, allegedly or some hireling of hers. If so one would assume that burglary ran like a hereditary disease in the Monk's Mead family, and that Julian, or someone acting on his behalf, had burgled Peter Barton's desk for the same reason several decades later. In that case it was possible that Julian was behind the kidnapping and had lured Barton to Sunningdale with a promise of fresh material for his thesis. He would need an intermediary, because an approach from anyone connected with Monk's Mead would have made Barton suspicious, knowing that information for his thesis was the last thing the Lindsays would let him have. Moreover, why Sunningdale?

She was becoming more and more convinced that the Stamford and Barton burglaries were the work of someone else hiding in the background, who had a long-term interest in the inner story of Anthony Mortlock. But was the same person responsible for beating up Julian twice in London, murdering his French visitor and trying to wreck the garden at Monk's Mead? If so, what was his motive?

She was driving very fast, for her next task was to read up everything that had been published about the goings-on at Bletchley Park during World War Two, and she was determined to get to Guildford in time to ransack the public library for books on the subject. Having managed this with minutes to spare, she drove back to Archerscroft Nurseries. Bill Wilkins was still there, closing up the glass-houses for the night.

"There's a pile of mail orders in the office the size of a house," he reported. "And there's slugs holding a mass pop festival in that fancy new hosta that's not got a name yet."

"Oh Bill, I'll sit up all night and process the mail orders, and I'll wage war on the slugs first thing tomorrow."

"It's been waged already. But oh Celia, what a headache you gave me with that Annie."

"What Annie?"

"You remember, the one in the Monk's Mead tea-barn that I lavished me charms on to satisfy your vulgar curiosity."

"My vulgar curiosity, as you call it, has just nosed out two burglaries, a kidnapping, and an Intelligence mystery dating back to World War Two."

"Oh Celia, you haven't! Come on, tell us."

"All in good time, your curiosity is just as vulgar as mine. What has your Annie done to upset you?"

"She keeps phoning and trying to date me."

"Surely you can defend yourself against female predators at your age?"

"Sure, but I can't make up me mind. She keeps saying she's something important to tell me, something that's happened at Monk's Mead. I think it's a con, but it might not be."

"Bill, you are to date her instantly, d'you hear?"

"I have already. Tomorrow night, couldn't bear not knowing."

"Splendid, if it's a con you can give her a good spanking."

"I tell them their breath smells, that always chokes them off."

"How charming, why girls fall for you I can't imagine. But as you're going to Monk's Mead anyway, I've another job for you. I want you to take my camera and pretend to be a tourist. You're to shoot off the camera like a mad Japanese at everything in sight, and I want each of the four gardeners in the forefront of a picture, so that I can find out which of them have criminal records."

He agreed, with some grumbling, then added: "Oh, there was a message. Someone called Colonel Fortescue wants you to ring."

98

When Charles Fortescue came on the line he was at his most pompous. He had put her enquiry about Pilot Officer Mortlock to the relevant department of the Ministry of Defence, but could tell her nothing.

"Why not, Charles? Can't they trace him?"

"They say he worked at an establishment covered by the Official Secrets Act. I can't tell you anything more."

"Why not?"

"It would not be in the public interest."

"Oh really Charles. Everything about Bletchley's been published, down to the colour of the wallpaper and the make of toilet roll."

"Bletchley? Who *told* you it was Bletchley?"

"Never mind, but it was."

"I neither confirm nor deny that the establishment in question was Bletchley, and I strongly advise you to drop this whole matter. You say you're making this enquiry on behalf of his family. Tell them that if I was free to speak, what I would say would not help them clear his name, on the contrary."

"Clear his name, Charles? Clear it of what?"

"Of desertion, among other things."

"He deserted from a safe desk job to join a fighting unit, and what d'you mean, 'among other things'? Did he do something frightful at Bletchley and run away before they threw him out?"

"Celia, I have nothing more to say to you."

"Poor Charles, I'm sorry to be a tease. Aren't you glad I wouldn't marry you, you'd have hated it."

It was three in the morning. Celia had spent the evening in her office, processing a huge pile of mail orders. She had then retired to bed with three books, all she could lay hands on at the library, about the Second World War Intelligence operation code-named Ultra, and its headquarters fifty miles north of London at Bletchley Park.

She already knew the story in general outline. Bletchley's secret had been kept for a quarter of a century after the war ended, but when security restrictions were relaxed in 1974 a friend of her parents who had worked there as a Wren had told her the story in outline. The nub of the matter was that several strokes of luck, some brilliant mathematics and the fact that the Germans were creatures of habit, had enabled British cryptographers, building on inspired pre-war work by Polish Intelligence, to penetrate the secret of the Enigma cipher machine, which was used throughout the German armed forces to encipher radio messages passing between the higher commands.

By exploiting this breakthrough, Bletchley had supplied the Allied commanders with a constantly updated picture of the enemy's intentions, his supplies of petrol and ammunition, the numbers of tanks and aircraft deployed on each front, the movements of military trains, the weather over bombing targets too deep in occupied Europe for Allied meteorologists to predict, at times even the positions of U-boat packs lying in wait for Atlantic convoys.

In theory, what the cryptographers did was impossible, for the odds against them were astronomical. The Enigma machine had a keyboard like a typewriter. Every time a key was pressed, an electrical impulse was released into its circuitry; and at the same time a set of wheels through which the impulse had to pass revolved against each other, so that no two impulses followed the same electrical path from the keyboard. When, say, BERLIN was typed and came out of the circuitry as QLIFAP, each of the letters in the enciphered version had been arrived at by a different tortuous route.

This was baffling enough, but there was more to it. It was possible when setting up the machine to scramble the alphabet yet further by connecting the 26 letters to each other electrically in pairs, which introduced a huge number of extra permutations. The wheels were detachable and could be reassembled in any one of sixty possible arrangements. Other complications raised the choice of routes in the circuitry through which a letter being enciphered could pass to a figure which, when laid out in full, had 88 digits.

Each branch of the German war machine, the air force, the army, the SS police, and so on, had its own set of wheel orders, pairings of the alphabet etcetera, in other words its own cipher key. Some of them had several. All the radio networks changed their key every night at midnight, so that a race against time developed at Bletchley in the early hours of every morning to break the new keys. The first break was usually in the main air-force key, which the cryptographers code-named "Red" and the intercepted messages were often deciphered at Bletchley almost as soon as the German addressee received them. Later in the day other keys would be broken, with increasing success as the war went on. One of the most striking aspects of the whole operation was the success with which the secret was kept. By 1943 the German High Command was alarmed and mystified by Allied successes in predicting and frustrating its strategy. It suspected treason, but never seriously doubted the security of the Engima cipher.

Stamford thought that Mortlock's "brainstorm" had been caused by something that happened during his service at Bletchley. What? Reading between the lines of the published accounts, Celia suspected that a lot of tension must have built up in a closed society of temperamental people, living in uncomfortable rural billets and working in shifts on secret work of the utmost importance. But was that all? According to the Memoir he had been at Bletchley from mid-1940 to July 1941. Could the crisis have been precipitated by some event recorded in the books scattered on her bed? She decided to look carefully at an episode which had caused much heart-searching at Bletchley, namely the intelligence handling of the series of bombing raids which the Germans code-named "Operation Moonlight Sonata". At that stage, early November 1940, the cryptographers had penetrated not only the "Red" air-force cipher but also one called "Brown". This was used by the technicians who set up the navigational beams on which *Kampf Gruppe 100*, the German Pathfinder unit, relied to guide the main bomber force on to its target. Thanks to this it often became possible to predict by mid-afternoon where the main bombing raid would be that night, and to alert civil defence, the night fighters and the anti-aircraft batteries.

But on the first night of the "Moonlight Sonata" series of raids, no warning identification of the target was issued, no preparations were made in advance and the German bombers inflicted a frightful death toll on the virtually defenceless city of Coventry. Next day a horrifying rumour spread round Bletchley: the target had been known, it was said, but Churchill had vetoed advance precautions in case the public began to wonder why fire engines, ambulances and civil defence teams began to converge on Coventry long before the Dorniers and Heinkels began to do likewise. If people put two and two together, the answer would be roughly correct. Churchill, it was rumoured, had let Coventry be martyrized to safeguard the secret of Ultra.

This suspicion must have taken deep root in the Bletchley consciousness, to judge from the many closely argued pages which all the writers on Ultra had devoted, three decades later, to refuting it in the greatest possible detail. What would have been the effect at the time on the mind of a young poet working there? Had it sown the seeds of disillusion which produced the brainstorm six months later? The course of the war in the following months would have deepened his disillusion. For instance, it was known from a decrypt of 30th April 1941 that Rommel's *Afrika Korps* was desperately short of fuel, armour, food and vehicles. Why had the British forces in the Middle East not attacked it? In May 1941 Ultra had given ample, detailed warning of Hitler's intention to grab Greece and mount an airborne invasion of Crete. Why had the attempt to block these moves been too little and too late? An impatient left-wing poet, knowing nothing of Britain's appalling weakness and the limited options that were open, might well have concluded that the priceless advantage of Ultra was being thrown away by strategic bungling.

Then in June 1941 Hitler had suddenly attacked Russia. This could have been the last straw that set off the "brainstorm" a month later. Mortlock had strong pro-Soviet sympathies, by the following spring he was cursing the "grey men" for not opening a Second Front to relieve the pressure in the East. One could imagine his despair in the first weeks after the Germans attacked, when they seemed to be bringing Russia to her knees. But was Stamford's information right? Did one have to assume that world history as seen from Bletchley was more than a background to the mental crisis? Surely the main ingredient must have been an upset in Mortlock's love life. His verse diatribes against the Dark Lady pointed to that, but what on earth had the Dark Lady done?

Giving up the attempt to solve this riddle, she pushed all the Ultra books off the bed and tried to sleep. But after lying awake for five minutes she was up again, seized by an uncontrollable urge to have another look at the Memoir. She collected it from downstairs, took it back to bed with her and re-read the passage in which "K——", *alias* Barbara Seymour, made her rose-tinted contribution to the picture of the brave, happy soldier-poet Anthony Mortlock:

After he left Bletchley he kept in touch with me through occasional telephone calls, though he never told me where he was stationed or what false name he had given when he enlisted. The Ministry of War Transport, for which I worked, had been evacuated to a northern seaside town, and though our hearts longed for a meeting, our reunion plans were frustrated time and again by the difficulties of travel in wartime. It was not until June 1942 that I waited excitedly on the platform as his train drew in and saw him waving from the carriage window. He was thinner and older-looking, but seemingly his usual cheerful, serene self, though as our time together went on, I sensed an undertone of seriousness beneath the little jokes we exchanged. He had no regrets, he said. His previous Intelligence work had been fascinating. But he was sure he had done the right thing in leaving it to older men and joining a combat unit.

We parted as we had met, in a crowded railway station. It was the last time I was to see him, as I waved from the platform. Did he have a premonition of the fate that awaited him a few weeks later, on the beach at Dieppe? Looking back afterwards I was sure of it. He had known all along that those few sweet days together were destined to be our farewell.

What, Celia wondered, was this heavily scented piece of romantic fiction covering up? A quarrel, followed by reconciliation and a passionate reunion on the eve of battle? Perhaps, but could one imagine Barbara Seymour, a future Justice of the Peace and Commander of the British Empire, climbing back meekly into bed with a man who had told her she was disgusting and had better lie down in her coffin and hope to be raped? The story of the reunion had obviously been lushed up to satisfy Mrs Mortlock's sentimental tastes, but there had to be some truth behind it. How otherwise could one account for the procreation of Adam Lindsay?

Pondering this question, Celia fell into a fitful sleep, from which the alarm clock wakened her sooner than she would have wished. After breakfast a quick reconnaissance in the frame yard and seedbeds revealed that a good many slugs had taken refuge elsewhere from the war waged against them among the hostas by Bill. When the staff arrived she gave orders that the survivors of his onslaught should be tempted with beer offered in jam jars buried flush with the ground. Slugs loved beer and probably preferred drowning in a state of delicious intoxication to eating slug pellets, which were anyway liable to poison birds instead. Having dealt with this and other matters, she went back to her office and rang the wife of the Miffield Professor of Nuclear Physics at Oxford University.

"Margaret? It's Celia Grant, Celia Stevenson that was."

"Celia! How are you?"

They spent some minutes bringing each other up to date on their own and their childrens' activities, and on the latest count of grandchildren. Then Celia got down to business.

"Margaret, when you were at Bletchley during the war, d'you remember a good looking young man called Anthony Mortlock, rather a heart-throb I imagine?"

"Sorry, no. There were well over a thousand people on the

payroll, and anyway I didn't work at the Park. I was servicing a battery of those damn bombes in a disused chapel near Milton Keynes."

The bombe was an electromagnetic contraption developed at Bletchley which performed, in an age devoid of microchips, calculations which today would be entrusted to a computer. Because they were essential and almost impossible to replace, they were not concentrated at Bletchley where one enemy air raid could have destroyed the lot, but dispersed in the surrounding countryside. They were used to test all the possible wheel orders and other variables, and to discover which of the possible arrangements matched what was known at Bletchley as the "menu", a passage of cleartext which the cryptographers believed the enciphered message to contain. The bombes did this at a speed astonishing in 1942, and if the cryptographers' hunch was right the bombe would sooner or later, after rejecting several hundred thousand other possibilities, discover the key used to encipher the message. When that happened the bombe would stop, and the Wren in charge of it would transmit its findings to Hut Six at Bletchley, whereupon the cryptographers would set up the key on an Enigma machine and decipher the rest of the day's messages enciphered in that key.

"Waiting for the damn things to stop was a crashing bore," Margaret reminisced. "I knew it was important, so every time I got a 'stop' I put a mark in the hatband of that silly hat that us Wrens had to wear. But they never told you anything you didn't need to know, so I had no idea what the bombe was in aid of or why it was important. Can you imagine, Celia, I'd been married to David for twenty years before he told me."

"You mean, your husband worked on Ultra?" said Celia. "I never knew that."

"Probably not, the whole thing was unmentionable for so long that one never got into the habit of mentioning it, but we met playing table tennis there in 1943. Celia, why d'you want to know about this Mortlock person?"

"There seems to be a mystery about him, and someone who's

been trying to find out about it seems to have been kidnapped."

"Goodness, how lurid."

"It is rather worrying, yes."

"Kidnapped? Are you sure?"

"No, that's the trouble. I don't want to make a fool of myself by rushing off to the police with a false alarm, that's why I'm making a few enquiries myself first, very quickly."

"I wonder if David could help you, he may have known Mortlock. He's in his study, I'll ask him."

Presently one of Britain's top nuclear physicists came on the line. "Was Mortlock a mathematician or a linguist?"

"A linguist. He had very good German."

"Ah, that explains why the name means nothing to me. I was in Hut Six among the mathematicians. We set up the menus for the bombes and produced decrypts of the messages. The linguists in Hut Three translated them into English and told Churchill and various interested generals and so on what the Germans were saying to each other. If Mortlock was a linguist, you should ask one of the Hut Three people."

"Unfortunately I don't know any of them."

There was a pause. "Margaret says there's a rather sinister background to all this."

"Yes. But it's very vague. I think someone's in quite serious danger, but until I have a bit more to go on I can't do anything about it."

"Look. Give me your phone number. I'll ring round a few people and ask them if they knew him. The trouble is, the Hut Three watch worked in shifts, they wouldn't necessarily know him unless they worked on the same shift. Wait though, when are we talking about? 1942? '43?"

"Summer 1940 to July 1941."

"Ah, early days, that makes it easier. I'll do my best and ring you back as soon as I can."

"George. Where's that list of the people who were in the garden at Monk's Mead that morning? I want to go through it again, see if we missed anything."

"We been through it three times already. There's no one on it has any connection with Robelin or any motive that we can see."

"Someone picked up that knife from the counter in the refreshment room. It could be a no-motive impulse job. A junkie who asked him for money and he said no."

"In that case what were Robelin and his junkie doing in part of the garden where they weren't supposed to be, on the wrong side of a locked door?"

"This is one hell of a case, George. I give up."

It was midday before the phone call Celia was waiting for anxiously came through. "Mrs Grant? I've found someone for you to talk to about Mortlock."

"Oh, thank you. Who?"

"Edward Townsend, one of the best brains in Bletchley, used to be a schoolmaster, head of German somewhere. Lives in Salisbury now, retired of course. No use phoning, he's eighty and a bit deaf, his wife took the call and relayed messages, so you'll have to go and see him. He'll be expecting you."

"And he knew Mortlock?"

"That's right, he was the head of his watch, he'll tell you the whole story, which I gather is quite interesting. Oh, and one other thing. This chap you're worried about, the one you think may have been kidnapped. Is his name Peter Barton?"

"That's right. How did you know?"

"I rang three other people for you before I struck lucky with Townsend. Peter Barton had approached all of them in the past month or so, asking for information about Mortlock. He'd also been down to Salisbury to see Townsend."

"Anthony Mortlock," murmured Edward Townsend in his thin, age-worn voice. "Poor fellow. Such a tragedy."

Salisbury Cathedral was framed in the window. There was a print of the dreaming spires of Oxford over the mantelshelf, which had a tobacco jar on it adorned with the arms of an Oxford college. Mrs Townsend had provided tea and wafer-thin sandwiches and withdrawn with ostentatious tact. The frail old man sat propped among cushions in a wing chair with a rug over his knees. He had the high forehead and temples of a scholar, and his deep-set eyes were still handsome.

After a long pause he spoke again. "That young fellow who came here . . . what was his name again?"

"Was it Peter Barton?" Celia prompted.

"That's right, Peter Barton. He'd found out a good deal from other sources before he came to see me."

"When was that?"

"About ten days ago. . . . How much of the story d'you know?"

"Nothing."

"Then I'd better begin at the beginning, hadn't I?"

He paused to collect his thoughts, then spoke in short bursts with rests between them to recover his breath. "Poor Mortlock. A first class brain. Such a loss. He'd have had a brilliant academic career. Great charm too. Everyone at Bletchley liked him. Especially the young women. Very good looking, you see. But he didn't go in for any hanky-panky with them. Oh no. There was a fiancée somewhere in the background."

"Yes," said Celia. "Her name's Barbara Seymour."

"Whenever our watch was off the rota for a few days he'd slip up to London to see her."

"To *London?*" Celia sat up sharply. "Are you sure?"

"Yes, I remember clearly. I worried about that. London was being bombed, you see."

"How often did he go?"

"Perhaps two or three times a month. Why do you ask?"

"I didn't think he saw her as often as that. I'm sorry I interrupted, do go on."

There was another long pause. "I think his tutor at Oxford recruited him for us. It was all done that way. The old boy network. People despise it but it works. It's the only way of getting the right chaps for a show like that."

"Why him in particular?" Celia asked. "He was very young for a desk job."

There was a reason, Townsend explained. Mortlock had

spent 1939 as a post-graduate student at Tübingen University, researching into the influence of Hölderlin on Wordsworth, which meant that his knowledge of German was right up to date. This was important because the language had been changing rapidly. At Hitler's insistence words with a Germanic root were being invented to replace those of impure, alien and decadent derivation from French or Latin. When war broke out there was a shortage of first rate academics who had experienced Nazi jargon on the spot, and the shortage was even greater if one excluded as security risks those whose residence in Germany had made them starry-eyed about Hitler. Mortlock, however, had impeccable left wing credentials.

"Everyone was left wing then in the universities," said Townsend. "It was the conventional wisdom of the time. But Mortlock took it very seriously, with him it went deep. That came out over the pact that Stalin had made with Hitler. Allied himself with that filthy gangster, hoping it would keep Russia out of trouble. Let Hitler run amok in Western Europe instead, that was the idea. Everyone was disgusted. Even the left. Mortlock wasn't. He defended Stalin. Blamed us. Said we'd refused the Russians an alliance. Didn't want to tie ourselves up with the Reds, he said, for fear of offending some nasty little right wing dictatorships in Eastern Europe and the Balkans.

"There was something in what he said. We argued a lot. Usually on the dawn shift. There was nothing much to do till Hut Six had broken 'Red' and started sending the decrypts across for us to process. He was fun to argue with, used his brains. Not like the party-line communists. They were just parrots. Said it was an imperialist war, put round leaflets telling our soldiers not to fight. That was during the winter, you understand. Nothing much was happening, except that we were being bombed and expected to be invaded at any moment. Then in the spring of '41 things began to move."

Celia knew the story already from her reading. The strategic picture, as revealed by Ultra, had begun to change. Units massed across the Channel stopped discussing invasion preparations in their radio traffic. The talk overheard by the Bletchley eavesdroppers was of arrangements for moving to the East. By the New Year, the German Air Attaché in Sofia, "ably assisted," he telegraphed, "by a staff of over 300 additional personnel", was reconnoitring and reporting on airfield facilities in Bulgaria, and a Luftwaffe Mission in Rumania had been told to ensure that the ground organization on airfields there was geared to receive a fleet of some 500 aircraft. Over the next few months Ultra decrypts concerning trains carrying air force stores and ammunition confirmed agent reports of a massive military build-up in the Balkans, ready for the invasion of Greece. This came in April, followed by the seizure of Crete.

Were these moves dictated by German economic interests, particularly Rumanian oil? There was an alternative theory, supported by a growing body of evidence, that Hitler was securing his southern flank before attacking Russia. But the evidence was not conclusive, and many Intelligence pundits refused to believe that even Hitler could be mad enough to embark on an eastern adventure while Britain was still undefeated. Then came the decisive piece of evidence.

"It was with relief and excitement," Churchill recorded in his Memoirs, "that towards the end of March 1941 I read an Intelligence report from one of our most trusted sources of the movement and counter movement of German armour on the railway from Bucharest to Cracow." Coupled with all the other pointers this northward movement of armour could mean only one thing. Operation Barbarossa, the attack on Russia, was on.

Repeated attempts to warn Stalin seemed to fall on deaf ears. But one more attempt was made when the storm was about to break. Sir Alexander Cadogan summoned the Soviet Ambassador, Maisky, to the Foreign Office. As Maisky recorded in his Memoirs:

Cadogan began to dictate from documents lying before him. 'On such-and-such a day two German motorized divisions passed through such-and-such a point in the direction of your frontier. . . . On such-and-such a day six German divisions were concentrated at such-and-such a point on your frontier. . . . During the whole of May there passed through such-and-such a point in the direction of your frontier twenty-five to thirty military trains a day. . . . On such-and-such a date in such-and-such a district bordering on your frontier there were discovered such-and-such a number of German troops and planes. . . .'

Cadogan told Maisky that Churchill wanted him to pass all this on urgently to Stalin. Maisky did. Four days later Stalin reacted. The Soviet news agency, Tass, issued a communiqué dismissing stories of Russo-German tension as "clumsy cooked-up propaganda". Within a fortnight, German planes were bombing Russian villages, which was Hitler's way of informing Stalin that he had declared war.

Suddenly, Mortlock's politics were no longer an academic debating issue. They mattered. "He was in despair," Townsend remembered. "Angry, too. We'd known the attack was coming, he said. Why hadn't we warned the Russians? I made a few enquiries. Told him we had. Gave him an account of that terrible Maisky interview with Cadogan. Why hadn't the Russians acted on the warning and mobilized? I said, because Stalin was pig-headed and didn't believe the warning. Why not, asks Mortlock, weren't they told that this wasn't just agents' reports? Stuff that could be wrong and even deliberately mischievous? Weren't they told that this was cast-iron evidence based on decrypts of German machine cipher traffic?

"They hadn't been told that. Most of our field commanders hadn't either, not at that stage. For security reasons. We fed them some credible fiction. 'A well-placed source in Berlin, which has hitherto proved reliable', that sort of thing. After a bit the generals had to be told the truth. The cover stories were getting so improbable, we were afraid they wouldn't take the intelligence seriously.

"Mortlock kept on and on about it. Had the Russians been let into the secret of Ultra? He had to be told 'no'. He hit the roof, said they must be. Mankind's hope of a better future lay in the Soviet system, Hitler must not be allowed to destroy it. We must give the Russians Enigma machines and the know-how. Then they could exploit Ultra for themselves.

"Things were looking bad for them. The German armies had driven deep into the country. Mortlock was making life hell for everyone. Any bit of bad news from the Russian front made him worse. Then after a fortnight someone high up took him aside. Told him something I hadn't known. Nor had anyone else if it wasn't their business. Bletchley was organized in these water-tight compartments, you see. You weren't told unless you needed to know. That was the rule. They broke it to shut him up. They told him why the Russians couldn't have Ultra.

"It was quite simple. Somewhere at Bletchley, in one of the outlying huts, people had been working on Russian ciphers. They were told to stop when the Soviet Union became an ally. But they'd found out a lot. Russian cipher security was lax. Also, they knew that the German cryptographers were busy too. They were reading Russian cipher traffic. There was a bunch of Ultra decrypts somewhere that proved it.

"If we let the Russians in on Ultra, they'd chatter about it on their command networks. The Germans would read the messages. They'd realize that Enigma had been penetrated. We'd lose the intelligence source that was our best hope of winning the war.

"That shut Mortlock up. But oh dear, they'd told him too late. He'd taken the law into his own hands. Gone round to the Soviet Embassy and told them. Maisky called at the Foreign Office in a fury. Said he knew we'd penetrated the German machine cipher, how dare we not share it with the only ally that was doing any fighting? Cadogan kept his head. Told Maisky he'd been conned by a practical joker. We had no Enigma, it was unbreakable. Only a first class agent network.*

"The Russians aren't fools. They didn't believe the stuff they were getting from us came from agents. It was too quick and detailed. They knew it had to be decrypts. So they bore us a grudge for holding out on them. Churchill was finding them

*This paragraph contains the only statements about the history of Ultra which are not based on published sources or the author's personal knowledge.

difficult enough to handle already, that made it worse. All because the top brass at Bletchley waited a fortnight before they told poor young Mortlock something he had no operational need to know.

"It was him, of course. Who else? One afternoon he was called out of the hut in the middle of his watch. He never entered Hut Three again.

"What was to be done with him? Court martial? If he denied it they'd never make it stick. And you try holding a court martial when half the people there can't be told what job the accused was doing, let alone who he told what about it. But one of the rules was, once you were at Bletchley you weren't let out. Afraid you'd blab if they didn't keep you under their eye. If you were a misfit they invented a stooge job for you and kept you away from secret information.

"That was what would have happened to Mortlock, but he wasn't the sort to stand for it. He wasn't going to sit there rotting till the end of the war. Gave them the slip, ran away. That worried them. I think they probably gave his family a bad time, questioning them. But they never got on his track."

"I believe he enlisted in the army under a false name," said Celia.

"Yes. Got himself posted double-quick to the Commandos too. That shows you what sort of a man he was. They were choosy. Didn't take just anybody.

"It was the final irony, him being killed in that raid on Dieppe. It was a military nonsense mounted under political pressure. Stalin was yelling for us to open a second front in the west, take the heat off him. Roosevelt's top priority was appeasing Stalin, so he kept bullying Churchill to give 'Uncle Joe' what he wanted. Then there was the British Communist Party. It was respectable now that Russia was our ally, it was orchestrating a 'Second Front Now' campaign. Hinting that Churchill and Co. weren't trying hard enough to win the war. He knew we hadn't the shipping or the resources, if we tried to invade Europe then it would be a disaster. But in the end he had to tell the generals to mount a token gesture across the Channel to keep all these people quiet.

"The Dieppe raid was cancelled once because of the weather, then remounted on a smaller scale. Going to the same place was madness. The Germans knew the target of the cancelled operation, and had time to strengthen the defences. The Navy said it wasn't risking ships close inshore to cover the landings with a bombardment. Plans to substitute an air bombardment were abandoned for some idiotic reason. A lot of other things about the battle plan were cock-eyed, but the real crime was sending in the Canadians. That was because of pressure from the politicians in Ottawa. They wanted their troops to see some action instead of giving their country a bad name by getting fighting drunk in the Aldershot pubs. None of them had ever seen a shot fired in anger. The result was a massacre.

"The two Commando units were sent in on the flanks, to blow up the gun batteries on the heights east and west of the town. Mortlock was with Number Four Commando. They got to their battery. Blew up all the guns and killed the crews. He must have died happy, believing he'd done his bit to help Stalin."

There was a long silence.

"Did he ever confess?" Celia asked. "Tell them he'd leaked the secret of Ultra to the Soviet Embassy?"

"I asked about that. No answer. It was the watertight compartments again. I didn't need to know."

SEVEN

"YOUR ZOMBIE BOY friend's not here then," said Bill Wilkins, glancing round the bar of the Six Bells as he and Annie met to keep their drinks date.

"Who can you mean? I don't have a 'zombie boy friend'."

"Oh Annie, you have. Old misery-face in the wet blanket that follows you around."

"Oh, him."

"Who is he then?"

She thought for a long time before she answered. "That's my husband."

"Married, are you?" He leapt up like a startled antelope. "What's the idea then, making me date you?"

"We're separated. I thought he'd stop pestering me if he saw me with an elegant new admirer."

"Oh no, Annie, you got it all wrong. That's not the way, it only makes them worse." He began downing his beer in great gulps. "Sorry love, I'm off out of here. I been had this way before. You're in a pub and a girl gives you the come on, and you don't fancy her no more than you would cold suet pudding, but next thing you know you're in a punch up with her husband who's a bricklayer with seven pints inside of him."

"A punch up? With my Fred? He's much too feeble, anyway it's his evening class tonight, in basketwork. Sit down, do."

"Look Annie, you're wasting me time and I'm wasting yours."

"No, wait. I didn't get you here because of Fred, there's something important I want to show you."

"Well show me then."

"It's not here, it's at Monk's Mead."

"Then tell us what it is. You don't get me trailing off there on a damn mystery tour."

"Very well, but sit down. I'm not telling the whole bar."

Listening to her story, Bill came to the unhappy conclusion that it would have to be investigated, though he still had grave doubts. "Okay, we'll go there and see. But look Annie, if this is a con I shall turn very, very naughty and sadistic."

"It's not a con. Wait till you see."

"Let's go then," said Bill. "But it better be good, or you'll be walking home."

Outside in the car park it was still light. "Why does it say 'Archerscroft Nurseries' on your van if you're a journalist?" Annie asked.

"They let me borrow the van," said Bill, too bored with the whole encounter to explain.

A car went past. He stared after it.

"Someone you know?" said Annie.

"Yes." It was Celia's car and she was driving very fast.

Celia was full of excitement. She knew now what Mortlock had meant when he accused his Dark Lady of "gifting away" his "tables": he had blabbed, unforgivably, to Barbara about Ultra and the need to share it with the Soviet Union. She was as full of pro-Soviet fervour as he was (hard to imagine but people were at the time). It was she who had leaked the Ultra secret to the Soviet Embassy without consulting him, thus bringing his Bletchley career to an inglorious end.

Celia drove past the Six Bells and on towards Monk's Mead. On her way back from Salisbury she had remembered a line of enquiry she should have explored long ago. By driving hell-for-leather she had arrived in time to follow it up before the hour became indecently late for a social call.

She had been shown into the sort of sitting room which is only sat in when visitors have to be impressed. It was also used for displaying silver-framed photographs of unbeautiful wedding couples. The brides bore an unfortunate family resemblance to Celia's bony nosed hostess, Mrs Hall, who was perching so rigidly on the edge of the upholstery that Celia felt bound to do likewise.

As an excuse for her intrusion she had invented a bedridden mother of ninety who, for lack of an affordable nursing home and in conformity with current social services doctrine, was being "cared for in the community" by Celia. The problem was to find someone who could sit with her when Celia had to go out. Could Mrs Hall help, by any chance?

"Who recommended me to you, Mrs er——?"

"Nobody, actually. I remembered reading about you in the paper. It was a report of an inquest."

Mrs Hall seemed to relish this. "That's right, on poor Mrs Mortlock."

"And I remembered that you lived near to Monk's Mead and used to help them out when they needed the same thing, so I thought I'd ask on the off-chance."

"I'm sorry, I don't do it as a regular thing. The Lindsays asked me, and as we're neighbours I said I'd oblige. Not that I got much thanks for it."

"I know, I've had some of this. One gets fond of the old person and even if the relatives aren't a bit grateful one carries on. Was she lucid right to the end?"

"Oh no, poor thing, she rambled a lot. All about how Julian, that's the son-in-law, had cheated her and treated her poor innocent daughter like dirt, and how she'd be revenged on him from beyond the grave."

"Oh dear, what nonsense, what can she have meant?"

"I don't know, it was all very confused. And there was a lot about some trust, and her grandson being a bastard. I didn't listen much, you couldn't make sense of it. I just got on with my knitting."

"There was another old friend that used to visit her a lot. A Miss Seymour, who gave evidence at the inquest."

"Oh her! You should have heard the old lady talk about Miss Seymour. It made me laugh sometimes, to hear her call that old stick of a schoolmistress a filthy whore."

"Old people do have strange fancies sometimes, don't they?"

117

"She did. Kept complaining about the food too, and the way the family treated her."

"Old people often do, it's understandable. I'm sure her daughter and son-in-law were very fond of her."

Mrs Hall pursed her mouth grimly. "They put on a lovey-dovey act when I was there, of course. But they killed her all right."

"How dreadful. I wonder why."

"For her money, I suppose. They gave her the sleeping pills and arranged to be out so she wouldn't be found till too late."

"I remember, there was a muddle about which day you were to come and sit with her. Which of them was it made the muddle?"

"Both of them. They must have planned it together."

"But which of them actually phoned you to arrange it?"

"That was him, but she was in it too. They hated her. It wasn't a mercy killing, I don't care what they said at the inquest."

Bill parked the van by the tea-barn at Monk's Mead and got out. The sun was setting behind the trees of the Wild Garden.

"Wait here," said Annie. She vanished, and came back with a spade. "You'll be needing this."

"Which gardener was it?" Bill asked.

"The oldish one with grey hair and a cleft chin. His name's George."

"What did he bury, you didn't see?"

"No, it was wrapped in one of those black plastic bags they have for dustbins. Something long and narrow. It could have been a weapon."

"What 'weapon'? The Frenchman was stuck with a knife they stole from the tea-barn, they left it in him and the police got it. There wasn't no 'weapon' left around for anyone to bury."

"I can't help that, I'm only telling you what I saw."

"Annie, you saw this George burying something next morning, the day after the murder. How come you never told the police?"

"It didn't register at first, gardeners are always digging. Then after a bit I wondered. What was he doing, putting a plastic bag in that hole?"

"But it was last week you phoned me to come and see. You should have gone to the police then, not waited around for me."

"I don't trust the police. They twisted my arm when I was demonstrating and they treated Fred disgracefully when he got drunk and broke a window."

This gets more unreal and creepy every minute, Bill thought. But having gone along with it so far, he decided to see it through to whatever lurid finish Annie had devised for him. He set off towards the entrance to the garden.

"No. This way, the gate's locked for the night," said Annie and led him along the wire fence to a point where the low branch of a tree overhung it. "No problem," she said, gripping the branch and swinging herself over. Bill followed, and they worked their way through undergrowth to one of the paths through the Wild Garden. Annie strode along it confidently, then paused.

"This is the place," she said.

"You're sure?"

"Yes. He planted that lily thing on top of the hole to mark it."

Bill moved the clump of *Crinum powellii* expertly out of the way and began to dig. He was expecting to find nothing, or at best something ridiculous, and was deciding what to say when this happened, when his spade encountered an obstacle. He dug round it carefully and pulled it out. As Annie had said, it was a plastic bag. It contained something that seemed to be flat and T-shaped. Freed from its wrapping it proved to be a white-painted notice board bearing the legend "GENTLEMEN", with a short stake attached for sticking it into the ground.

Bill stared at it. So it was a con after all. "Funny funny joke," he snapped. "So why don't I turn you up and spank you?"

She was staring too. "It's not my fault, I don't understand this," she protested.

"Listen Annie, I'm sick of your play-acting and I hate crazy little tarts trying to make themselves important — "

"Be quiet, let me think. I know what must have happened. It's George's doing, I'm sure that's it, he's played a trick on me."

"And I'm the Fairy Prince and you're Snow White and if I could turn you into a frog and tread on you I would."

She clutched his arm and pointed. "Look! Someone's coming."

He turned. A dim figure was hurrying towards them in the twilight, now clearly visible, now out of sight among the trees. Bill thought rapidly. It was probably George, arriving to give the next twist to whatever drama this little lunatic had mounted. He thrust the notice board and its plastic bag into a clump of azaleas, plumped the *Crinum powellii* back into its hole and strode away to put a thicket of rhododendrons between him and the enemy. Annie followed him, still apologizing and claiming not to understand.

"Stop that damn chatter or he'll hear us," he hissed.

But it was too late. Footsteps crashed through the undergrowth, homing on the noise she was making, and halted on the far side of the rhododendron clump. Heavy breathing could be heard, interrupted by muffled curses.

"What ho within there," cried a high tenor voice. "Yoo hoo."

"Oh my God it's Fred," said Annie, "and he's drunk again."

"Aren't I a n-nice surprise?" Fred went on. "How, you ask, did I get into this garden of d-dainty delights? 'With love's light wings did I oerperch these walls, for stony limits cannot hold love out'. Romeo and Juliet Act Two Scene Two."

"He teaches English at a grotty little boy's prep school," Annie explained, "when he's sober."

"Your new gentleman friend is with you, I b-believe," Fred called. "His van is in the car park."

"Take no notice, it only encourages him," said Annie.

"Coo-ee, I can see you," chanted Fred loudly. "The hair-do of your peroxided paramour shines through the shrubbery like a good deed in a naughty world."

Bill ducked his blond head and decided that if Celia ever sent him on an errand like this again, he would wear a hat.

120

"Come on out, both of you," Fred yelled at the top of his voice, then added more quietly, "when you have adjusted your dress, of course."

"They'll hear him up at the house and call the police," said Annie anxiously. She broke cover and began telling Fred to keep quiet in an increasingly loud undertone, till she was making as much noise as he was and the air rang with a slanging match of abuse. They were enjoying themselves, Bill decided. They reminded him of some actors he had seen with his girl friend in a London theatre club, improvising themselves into a state of happy hysteria. Seeing no point in staying around, he crept away anti-clockwise round the rhododendron clump, only to collide with Annie, hurrying round in the opposite direction with Fred, protesting loudly, in tow.

"He mustn't be found in here," Annie urged. "Help me to get him out."

"Will I hell. Dump him. I'm getting meself out."

"Leggo of me," Fred complained in a high-pitched whine.

"Shut up, you nerd," said Bill and pushed him not too gently in the chest. He collapsed peacefully into the undergrowth and lay there, moaning faintly.

It was quite dark. The noise had raised the alarm. Bobbing flashlamps appeared at various points in the Wild Garden and voices echoed. Bill ran as fast as he could in what he hoped was the direction of the boundary fence, but encountered a high brick wall. A quick search revealed a wrought iron gate leading into the Long Borders, dimly visible in the darkness. The only obvious exit was dangerously near the lights of the house, so he withdrew into the Wild Garden again and stopped to listen and look. The action and the flashlamps were concentrated at a spot near the clump of rhododendrons. Fred had been found. They were questioning him. There was no sign of Annie.

The boundary fence had to be somewhere on his right. Moving as quietly as possible, he went in search of it. But the pattern of paths was confusing and by the time he glimpsed it dimly a line of three flashlamps was advancing steadily, like beaters at a shoot. The fence was chest-high and there was no overhanging tree to help, but unless he acted quickly he would be trapped against it by the search party. He flung himself against it and tried to scramble over.

As he struggled a car drove into the car park and swung round so that he was caught in its headlights. A door slammed and a woman's voice shouted: "Here they are, Julian. Now. We've caught you. Who are you and what are you doing in there?"

"It's all right, Lady Lindsay," said Annie's voice from along the fence. "It's only me. Annie from the tea-barn."

"What are you doing here at this time of night? Who's that with you? Julian, where are you? She's got a man with her."

"I'm here," said a deep voice behind Bill. "Put your hands above your head, whoever you are, and don't move."

Bill obeyed. There was no point in arguing with a loaded shotgun.

"I had to hand it to that Annie," Bill told Celia over a whisky late that night. "She's a fantastic liar. Ooh Lady Lindsay, she says, ooh Sir Julian, me friend and me was ever so worried. We happened to drive into the car park and, oh dear, we was horrified, there was Fred's bike propped against the fence and him inside the garden carrying on and drunk as per usual, it's a mystery how he got in there in that state. She was separated from him, she said, but she didn't want him to come to no harm, and what with all the vandalism there's been in the garden, and him having been in trouble with the police once before, he'd be accused of doing the damage if he was caught in there and he'd be in real bad trouble. So me and me friend was trying to get him out, she says."

"And they believed that?" Celia asked.

"Not at first they didn't. They got us into the house, Sir Julian and the son, Adam, is that his name? And Sir Julian kept picking up the phone to call the police and putting it down again, to frighten us, that was, and make us talk. Lady Lindsay kept asking what business had we in the car park, anyway, why did we 'happen' to drive in there and 'happen' to see Fred's bike propped against the fence? So Annie said we'd gone in there to snog in the car, only she had a polite name for it, and Adam said 'what a strange coincidence' in a strangled sort of voice, I think he was bursting his guts trying not to laugh. And the girl, Adam's daughter, what was her name?"

"Tessa."

"She was real nasty to Annie and said hadn't she enough of a headache with Fred and she must be subnormal to lumber herself with me as well. Next thing, Sir Julian asked me who I was, and I got in quick before Annie could invent anything silly and said I was your head gardener. That calmed him down a bit, but he kept looking from me to Annie and wondering what such a well set up specimen of manhood wanted with a girl that looked like a panic-stricken rat from a laboratory, and Lady Lindsay was sorry for Annie, partly because of me lustful intentions in the car park, but more I think because of dismal old Fred hanging around her like a sort of helpless human limpet. By this time Sir Julian had decided me and Annie was probably telling lies, but only to cover up for Fred, so he concentrated on him, saying what was he doing in the garden if he wasn't there to wreck it, which was silly because anyone could see poor Fred was in no state to wreck a window-box, let alone a ten-acre garden. But he went on and on about it, what was Fred doing in the garden if he wasn't a big-time criminal and so on, but luckily Fred was too far gone to speak and invent a silly answer. In the end he said 'Now I really shall ring the police' and Lady Lindsay said 'No dear, think for a moment', and there was an ugly great silence with them two goggling at each other, like two dogs wondering whether to fight. Creepy, that was."

"She's terrified of publicity about the damage to the garden," Celia explained. "Police means a fuss, and a fuss might lead to publicity, that's why she wanted to keep them out of it. Sir Julian wanted to make maximum fuss about Fred, and build him up as a suspected vandal, because for reasons I don't understand, suspicion must be kept away from the gardeners. So he wanted the police in. Which of them won?"

"Neither, it was a draw. Sir Julian got so mad at Fred that he took a grip on him and shook him, but Fred's stomach was in too delicate a state to be shook and it started him off puking gallon after gallon of beer on their nice carpet, I thought he'd never stop. And that was the only sensible thing Fred did all evening, because they was all so disgusted with his mess that they bundled the three of us out of the house and no more questions asked, but would we get rid of Fred at once. So I fetched the van round from the car park and shovelled him in, and dropped him on his doorstep to sleep if off. Then I dropped Annie at her place and gave her a piece of me mind and told her to keep out of me sight unless she wanted me to take a hairbrush to her bottom."

"All seems to be well that ends well," Celia decided, "except for one snag. What happens in the morning when someone at Monk's Mead finds a plastic bag and a notice saying 'Gentlemen' lying beside an uprooted *Crinum powellii* in the Wild Garden?"

"They won't, I've took care of that. I nipped over the fence again on me way back here and replanted the crinum and tidied it all up nice. The notice board's in the van."

Celia was so intrigued that she went out to the van to look. She came back puzzled and thoughtful. "That notice board must mean something. But I don't know what."

"It means 'I am a nympho but no rough trade please, only gentlemen, signed Annie'."

"No really Bill, you have nymphos on the brain. You've met her, I haven't. Is she completely mad?"

"Half and half, I'd say. She can think when she has to, look how she talked us out of that fix."

"Exactly, so would she really choose an object to bury that would make her look damn silly when you dug it up? Why not something interesting like a bloodstained knife?"

"Are you saying it wasn't her buried it?" Bill asked. "Who then?"

"George. Those gardeners are up to no good. When she says she saw him doing it she was telling the truth."

"Why would a gardener that's up to no good bury the notice from the gents' toilet?"

"I can't imagine. Where is the gents', anyway?"

"Round the back of the barn where they have the tea."

"Is there a notice missing?"

"I dunno Celia, I found it easy enough the other day when I was there."

"We must look. Damn, I don't see where the wretched thing fits in, I shan't sleep a wink tonight. I'm worried about Mary Lindsay and there's this unfortunate young man who's been kidnapped, and none of the pieces in this whole mad puzzle fit together."

"Oh Celia, you're no use to the business while you're in this state. Come on now, tell me all the things that don't fit, and we'll muck them around till they do."

"Bless you, Bill, you are a comfort. Very well, let's start with old Mrs Mortlock. According to Mrs Hall who used to sit with her sometimes, she was senile and rambled incoherently. But according to her family, she was perfectly lucid. What d'you make of that?"

"The family's lying. They make out she decided to die and got the pills somehow and took them. That story looks a bit dodgy if she was loony as a kite."

"There's another possibility, I can't make up my mind which is right. We know something pretty weird happened back in '40 and '41. She's kept it to herself all these years, and now she's ninety and it preys on her mind and the controls begin to break down and she starts to talk about it. Only it's so weird that Mrs Hall mistakes what she says for senile ramblings."

"Oh yes, Celia, I see what you mean. And the family say 'what if she blabs it all to the vicar and the doctor and all the dear old friends who come with the flowers and the grapes, oh dear what a problem!' So the answer's an overdose."

"Yes, except that 'the family' isn't the right expression. Adam and Tessa aren't in on the secret, it happened before they were born and they're as baffled as we are. But Barbara Seymour is, she was involved in the wartime goings-on and according to Mrs Hall the alleged 'ramblings' were all about how wicked Barbara and Julian were. Darling Mary seems to have figured as their victim."

"That's right, she would be," said Bill. "She's the clueless victim type."

"I agree. But what baffles me is, if Julian and Barbara are the villains and Mary got the rough end of the stick, and if Mrs Mortlock knew it, why did she say God bless you my children and let Mary marry Julian? That happened a year after the crisis over Anthony."

"Simple," said Bill. "She didn't know how wicked they'd been, not then. She didn't cotton on till later."

This left Celia thunderstruck, it was so obvious. "That's it, I was a moron not to spot it. Mrs Mortlock commissions Andrew Stamford to write the Memoir, he puts out an appeal for letters and reminiscences of darling Anthony, and in come a lot of filthy poems that have to be suppressed, plus clear evidence of villainy by Barbara and Julian."

"And then she gets the lawyers along to stop wicked Julian from letting the garden go to ruin and putting his fingers in the cash box."

"Yes, that fits. She set up the trust in the same year the Memoir was published. But Mary's marriage seemed to be working out reasonably well. She seemed to be as happy as she was capable of being, so why wreck her marriage and make her miserable by telling her what Julian had done? Mary doesn't know, that's obvious from her behaviour."

"And Julian and Barbara had to slip her the pills quick, before Mrs Mortlock let the cat out of the bag to Mary."

"Well, Mary would be the last person she'd tell after keeping it from her all those years, but there is a risk, yes. If she's started talking about it to strangers, her inhibitions may break down even further so that she tells Mary, that's another reason for doing something."

"Which of them does the murder? Him or Barbara?"

"Goodness knows. They both have alibis of a sort, but they may not be watertight."

"My money's on Barbara. She's in and out all the time with the flowers and the grapes, so why not the knock-out pills too?"

"Why not indeed. But, oh dear, Barbara's the worst headache of the lot. Nothing about her fits."

"For instance?"

"If you believe her own story, she was the great romance of Mortlock's life, they were soul-mates right up to his death at Dieppe. There's a nostalgia-drenched paragraph by her in the Memoir about how he went up to Blackpool for a farewell reunion shortly before the raid, and one is left to infer that this is why Adam was born nine months later and adopted by Julian and Mary, who got married with four months to spare. That's what you might call the Authorized Version, but it doesn't match the facts. Mortlock stopped writing nice poems to Barbara after the crisis at Bletchley and started writing her very nasty ones, including one which accused her in veiled terms of having leaked the Ultra story to the Soviet Embassy. As for the alleged scenes of passion in Blackpool, can you imagine any woman, let alone a future Justice of the Peace and headmistress of a famous girls' school, climbing back meekly into bed with an ex-lover who'd told her to lie down in her coffin and hope to be raped by a passer-by? I can't, and another thing: his chief at Bletchley, a man called Townsend, swears that Mortlock used to rush away to a 'fiancée' in London whenever he had a day or two off. Barbara wasn't there. Her Ministry had been evacuated to Blackpool."

"No problem, two girls at once," said Bill promptly.

"But wouldn't you expect him to write one or two nice poems to girl number two, as well as this stream of absolutely foul ones to Barbara? Suppose it wasn't a girl in London, but something else rather sinister?"

"What sort of a sinister thing, Celia?"

"Oh dear, how do I know?"

He brooded for a long time. "I can think of something a bit sinister, if you can make sense of it."

"Yes? What?"

"*Julian isn't okay.*"

127

Celia sat up sharply. "Oh, nonsense. He got married in his early twenties in the middle of a world war, you'd have to be straight to do that."

"I don't care what he did. I've seen spiral staircases straighter."

"Bill, I know you're good at telling, but are you sure?"

"Dead sure, you can tell from how they look at you. All the time we was in that house tonight he was looking at me in that special way they have and then at Annie, and saying to himself, Well, if he's so dead keen on it that he had to go snogging with that sad little piece in a car park, he's a long way from my side of the fence."

"But a man in his position. Think of the risk of scandal."

"I'm not saying he'd start anything risky, not now, maybe he hasn't for years, he was only window-shopping. But remember, Mortlock's supposed to have been his best friend. That's when the scandal was, back then."

It took Celia some minutes to come to terms with this. "But what about the great outpouring of love poems to Barbara Seymour?"

"I dunno about them. Where's the book, let me have a see."

He hunted backwards and forwards through the book, pausing at the love poems and muttering: "Who says all these are about Barbara? It's *your* voice, *your* this, *your* that, you and your all the time, never she or her. Are the black poems the same? Nothing to say whether it's a man or a woman?"

"Yes, they're the same," said Celia, thinking back. "There's nothing in the third person."

He went back to the book. "Look at this one, about the anniversary and how glad he was that they'd teamed up. See how it begins:

'When my secret hand met yours . . .'

That's not a man making it with a girl, it's two blokes fumbling and groping to find out if the other's game for what they could both have gone to prison for back in 1940."

Celia thought about this for a long time before she said:

"Bless you Bill. You're right, the statue clinches it. I couldn't make out what the point was of dressing it up in women's clothes."

"Oh yes Celia, that fits, they were making Mortlock out to be a transvestite. What about the piglet though?"

"It could have been meant for Adam, but why did they cut its head off?"

"They could have thrown it in just for the hell of it, to disgust everyone. They're nasty people, and mad."

Nasty people, Celia thought, but with a definite aim behind their madness, she had been sure of this all along. What had baffled her was guessing what the aim was. Now she knew. Or rather, she had an overpowering hunch.

"Bill, can you manage without me tomorrow? I must go up to London early, there are things I ought to check at once."

EIGHT

CELIA WAS QUIETLY pleased with herself as she walked out of the Central Registry of Births, Deaths and Marriages in Kingsway, from which she had just extracted an interesting birth certificate. It related to Christopher Julian Henry Lindsay, who seemed to have dropped his first baptismal name like a hot potato and described himself in *Who's Who* as "Lindsay, Sir Julian Henry". She had never been happy about "Kit" being short for "Kitten". "Christopher" made much more sense.

It was easy to imagine what had happened when the news of Anthony Mortlock's death reached Monk's Mead in the late summer of 1942. For obvious reasons he had told his parents nothing of his unorthodox love-life, and when his mother found unpublished love-poems addressed to 'Kit' among his effects, she was determined to hunt out and meet the girl who had captured her beloved son's heart. His undergraduate friends had never heard of a girl called Kit, so she made enquiries among such later wartime friends as she knew of. One of them, Christopher Julian Lindsay, heard of this and was alarmed. There was a risk of her discovering who 'Kit' really was, and that, in the censorious sexual climate of 1942, could have turned out awkwardly for the career prospects of an ambitious young man. But, much more serious, Mrs Mortlock might stumble on the fact that the love affair had ended in an almighty row, with her Anthony circulating abusive poems about Julian to their joint acquaintance and accusing him of peddling Intelligence secrets to the Soviet Embassy. The scandal had to be suppressed, Julian decided. Someone must equip Anthony in retrospect with a respectably heterosexual love affair.

Someone, but who? There was one obvious candidate:

Julian's Cambridge contemporary and friend Barbara Seymour. Her family home was a few miles from Monk's Mead and
she had met Anthony once or twice, so it was a plausible
romance to invent. But how could he persuade Barbara to
agree?

At this one could only guess, but all would be explained if
Barbara, when approached with this proposition, had recently
discovered to her dismay that she was pregnant. The idea of
pretending that Mortlock was the father would have seemed
attractive. To be carrying the child of a dead war hero would be
a much more elegant state of affairs than to be 'in trouble' after,
for instance, a sordid intrigue in Blackpool with a married man
separated by wartime circumstances from his wife. Moreover,
the Mortlocks had money. So she agreed, and with Julian's help
concocted for Mrs Mortlock's consumption an account of her
imaginary romance with Anthony. This naturally included an
opportunity for the necessary night of rapture in Blackpool to
account for her condition.

So far so good. But Barbara was an ambitious young career
woman, with no wish to be lumbered with an illegitimate child
to look after. Nor could she dispose of the infant unobtrusively
through the good offices of an adoption society if Mrs Mortlock
was to be told that it was her grandchild. There were the child's
interests to consider, what would be best for it? By far the
neatest solution, she decided, would be for someone to marry
Mrs Mortlock's daughter Mary and adopt it, and why should
not that somebody be Julian?

Having asked Barbara to lie like a trooper on his behalf,
Julian was hardly in a position to refuse, and anyway it seemed
quite a good idea. By marrying he would distance himself from
the breath of homosexual scandal. Mrs Mortlock was rich and
Mary was now her sole heiress. She would be stuck at Monk's
Mead in attendance on her mother and the garden, and his
work in Whitehall would provide him with excuses for no-
questions-asked nights away in London. So he duly wooed and
won Mary, and one could imagine Mrs Mortlock's delight at an
arrangement which provided her at one stroke with a grandson

and a husband for her awkward and not very marriageable daughter; a husband, moreover, who had been her dear boy's best friend.

Then, in 1947, came the explosion. Andrew Stamford, who had been gathering material for the Memoir, brought her what had come in as a result of his appeal for letters and reminiscences about Anthony. There were some items which puzzled him. Could she provide an explanation?

The explanation was only too clear. She had been conned. Barbara had lied, there had been no love affair with Anthony, four-year-old Adam was not her grandson. Her son and her son-in-law had been lovers. On the evidence of the black poems, and the explanations of them that Stamford had been able to collect, Julian was somehow responsible for Anthony's leaving Bletchley under a cloud. Though the details were wrapped in official secrecy, it seemed that Anthony had been accused of leaking secret Intelligence matters to some unauthorized person. In fact he had confided them to Julian, who had done the leaking.

What was she to do? Create a rumpus? Tarnish the image of her dead son, a poet-hero of the Second World War? Unthinkable. Disillusion her timid, insecure daughter about the husband she still doted on, and make her divorce him? Preferably not. He seemed to be behaving fairly well and a signed confession, safely deposited with lawyers in London, would ensure that he continued to do so. It was a pity that Adam was not a Mortlock after all, but he had the advantage of being male. If she kept quiet there would eventually be two robust men to help poor dear Mary secure the future of the garden in years to come.

What was to be done about the Memoir? All her friends knew it was being worked on. So did a growing number of admirers of Anthony's poetry. To cancel the Memoir would be to admit that the research had unearthed discoveries too discreditable to publish. She would stand over Stamford with a shotgun and make him go ahead with a heavily sanitized version. Even the rubbish Barbara had written would have to go in, because she had been paraded around the district as the beloved who had been immortalized in verse. It was all very regrettable, but Mrs Mortlock belonged to a generation which valued surface respectability. There was no alternative. She must keep quiet.

Filled with pity for Mrs Mortlock, Celia took a bus to Victoria Station and was waiting at the ticket barrier when the train from Guildford drew in at the platform. Tessa, Adam and Bill Wilkins got out. As far as Monk's Mead knew, Tessa was at her dentist's and Adam was attending a dahlia show at the Royal Horticultural Hall, but the real aim of their journey was different. Thanks to a busy morning of research Celia knew the answer to the Monk's Mead riddle, but the police had to be persuaded that she was right and prodded into action. Once before she had been held up to public ridicule for going to the police with an unlikely story which proved in the end to be correct. Taking no chances this time, she would present herself at Scotland Yard at the head of an imposing array of witnesses, to corroborate what she intended to say.

Before proceeding up Victoria Street to New Scotland Yard, she briefed the others on her discoveries.

"This is like an opera libretto in reverse," Adam commented when she had finished. "Instead of finding a long lost parent, I have mislaid one and become a genetic riddle."

Tessa was still smarting at having been treated as a half-mad nuisance by the Sunningdale police, and she fretted for action to rescue Peter Barton. Bill was fidgeting too, impatient to get this over, hurry back to Archerscroft and catch up with arrears of work there.

Celia was a mass of nerves, and quaked inwardly as she approached the reception desk at New Scotland Yard. Her past experiences with the police had been alarming, one never knew which way their minds would jump. Could they be persuaded to act before yet more death and destruction fell on Monk's Mead?

Inspector Matthews was unhappy. His breakfast had disagreed with him. It being August, he was snowed under with the work of colleagues on holiday as well as his own. He was sweating like a pig, for New Scotland Yard had been built at a time when architects had a mania for smothering their buildings in glass, and his south-facing office was an oven. Moreover he was being persecuted on the internal phone by his least favourite colleague, Inspector Barrington of the Forgeries Squad, a show-off with a hair-cut so trendy that he looked like a forgery himself.

"I have four people in my office," Barrington cooed, "whom I think you ought to see."

Then damn you for phoning me in front of them, Ted Matthews thought, instead of going into another room and finding out if I want to see them.

"I'm up to my neck," he growled. "What's it about?"

"A matter that concerns your department rather than mine."

"Then why the hell are they not in my office rather than yours?"

"Ah, a good question. One of them, a Mrs Grant, asked to see me in the first instance because she knew I would vouch for her as a reliable person. She was involved to some extent in the Armitage art forgery case, when that Dutch art expert got killed."

"Okay, then put them all in an interviewing room and I'll come down when I can."

"Good. I'm sure you'll be interested in what Mrs Grant has to tell you. Despite her charming exterior she is a person of great intelligence."

And why the hell shouldn't she be, Ted Matthews thought, having had dealings with several women with charming exteriors who had committed highly intelligent crimes. But when he had finished what he was doing and gone down to the interviewing room, he saw what Barrington meant. Mrs Grant was indeed pretty, but looked as capable of serious intellectual effort as Little Miss Muffet. With her was a blond chorus-boy whom she introduced not very believably as her head gardener, also a hawk-faced man in his forties and his handsome daughter, a Mr and Miss Lindsay.

"Quite a delegation," he grumbled.

"Yes," said the silver-haired Miss Muffet. "I thought it would help if I brought along some witnesses."

This was all very well, but four people would take longer to get rid of than one.

"Our information concerns Sir Julian Lindsay," she went on. "He is the head of Mr and Miss Lindsay's family and a former Permanent Secretary of the Ministry of Trade and Industry. When he retired he took a directorship in the private sector, and we believe he is being blackmailed into passing the firm's secrets to a third party."

"That's not a police matter," said Ted Matthews, relieved. "You should contact the security officer of the firm concerned."

"Except that the firm makes things like control equipment for guided missiles which are sensitive from the defence point of view."

This tiny self-possessed woman was getting on his wick, but her allegation had to be gone into seriously. "Have you evidence of this?"

"My stockbrokers are usually well-informed," she said and handed him a typewritten letter.

Dear Mrs Grant,

In answer to your telephone enquiry this morning, RGP Electronics is a firm started in 1980 by Mr R. G. Patterson, who was formerly a production manager at EMI. Under his direction it has since expanded rapidly and has succeeded in attracting a number of Ministry of Defence contracts. It produces sophisticated electronic control gear for specialist applications, including control gear for guided missiles, and seems likely to become a leader in this field. The ordinary shares stand today at 92 on the Unlisted Securities Market, and a purchase at that price might prove advantageous. You should remember, however, that investment in a firm which is the creation of one individual, and depends heavily on him for its continued profitability, must be considered highly speculative.

Sir Julian Lindsay joined the firm's board in July last year as Director with special responsibility for relations with government departments.

As instructed, we are holding this letter for you to collect from our reception desk later today.

Yours etc . . .

Matthews handed the letter back with a resigned sigh. Little Miss Muffet was probably a nut case, but it would take time to make sure.

"You're making a very serious allegation against a distinguished public servant," he said. "What evidence have you to support it?"

"It depends on what you call evidence. There's been a murder and a kidnapping and a lot of malicious damage, and I have some photographs you may care to see." She spread them out on the desk in front of him. They were studies of four men, taken unawares while standing about in a flower garden.

"These are the gardeners at Monk's Mead, Sir Julian's country home," she explained. "At least two of them are in the pay of the blackmailer and may have criminal records, perhaps you could check."

Ignoring the pictures, Matthews said: "Perhaps you'd just tell me first what happened."

He had addressed Little Miss Muffet, but the others chipped in to corroborate what she said. He found himself listening to a confused, collectively told story of treasonable activity back in 1941, of a baby fathered on the wrong man and an old lady's suspect death, of Sir Julian being beaten up in London and hiding the fact from his family, of vandalism and dead cats in the Monk's Mead garden.

"This story doesn't hang together," he interrupted. "What you're saying is, Sir Julian commited a treasonable act in 1941, and he's suddenly being blackmailed about it now, all these years later. Why the long gap?"

"We don't know there was a gap," said the astonishing Miss Muffet. "He may have been passing state secrets to the blackmailer throughout his Civil Service career."

"Then why is he refusing now to give the blackmailer what he wants? According to you he's being pressurized because he's dug his heels in and won't play any more. Why not?"

"You see, Inspector, Sir Julian isn't in the Civil Service any more. I imagine that in a smallish private firm that's well run, trade secrets are easier to protect and anyone leaking them stands a far worse chance of being found out. We think Sir Julian is refusing to provide the blackmailer with what he wants because the risk to him is too great."

Damn her, she has an answer to everything, he thought and tried another tack. "What proof have you that it's the gardeners doing the vandalism?"

"I caught one of them at it," said Adam Lindsay, "a man called Martin Blake. He was poisoning a flower border and I made Sir Julian sack him. He did, very unwillingly, but re-engaged him a few days later. The blackmailer had told him that sacking his tormentors wasn't allowed."

"Told him in no uncertain manner," said the tiny lady, "by choosing a visitor to the garden at random and murdering him on Sir Julian's doorstep. It was a horrifying, brutal way of saying 'don't sack the gardeners, don't step out of line.'"

"Oh come, Madam. You're telling me the blackmailer killed a totally innocent person to frighten Sir Julian into re-employing a sacked gardener?"

"Yes, the man's mad. Don't look at me like that, it's the only possible explanation. The victim was a Frenchman called Robelin. The Surrey police can find no connection whatever between him and the Lindsays and no reason why anyone should want to kill him. Besides, look at the timing: Martin Blake was sacked three days before the murder. Twenty-four hours after it he was back at work."

Matthews had read something about a Frenchman being murdered in a Surrey garden and tried to remember the details. But the effort of memory made his eyes glaze over, and the tiny lady had noticed. She was suddenly transformed into a red-faced Queen of the Fairies having a tantrum.

"You really must take this seriously, Inspector. We're

dealing with a sadistic madman, I shudder to think what he'll do if he isn't stopped. For goodness sake look properly at these pictures, this one is of the sacked and reinstated gardener who calls himself Martin Blake, though that's probably an *alias*. And this one who calls himself George Green was an accomplice in Robelin's murder. I expect they both have criminal records, will you *please* stop looking at me as if I was mad and go and check?"

Matthews found himself looking at a head-and-shoulders picture of a man with iron-grey hair and a cleft chin, photographed against an out-of-focus flower border. "Have you any evidence that this man was an accom — "

"Yes, we have," she snapped. "He was seen burying a piece of evidence, something used to commit the crime, and Mr Wilkins here dug it up. Show him, Bill."

The blond head-gardener dived under his chair and produced an awkwardly tied parcel, which he began to unwrap.

With an enormous effort, Celia managed to get her temper under control. "It was very ingenious," she began. "The sort of thing that only a very clever madman would think of . . ."

"Crikey George. If I could kick meself hard on the bottom I would and no mistake."

"Me too, I feel so bloody stupid."

"Fancy us wasting all that time checking on bloody Robelin."

"And asking the French about that Bruay-en-Artois nonsense of Sir Julian's."

"Instead of thinking about how Robelin had pissed his pants and how he smelt of beer."

"It was damn clever, when you think. He walks into that little yard with the bushes in, and there stuck in a flowerbed is the Gents' notice, next to the door in the wall. He's getting uncomfortable after all that beer, so when he sees the notice he says 'thank God for that' and goes through the door, and before you can say knife — Hell, I got knives on the brain."

"Hey, but what happens if it's not a man coming in there by himself that sees the notice? A couple, say, and he says to her 'wait here while I have a leak'? When he doesn't come out undamaged, she'll tell the police

how the trick was worked."

"That's the clever bit. Someone's loitering in front of the Gents' notice, hiding it. He waits till a man comes along by himself and there's no one else in the little yard, then he steps aside and lets the notice be seen."

"Who is he, a gardener?"

"No, we checked on them, they were all at their posts looking out for vandals, they had to have an alibi. It was a member of the public, admiring the bushes in there, and there was another member of the public ready with the knife on the far side of the door, hiding behind that big cactus thing. The gardeners copied the key for them so they could unlock the door, that's all."

"Except that George buried the Gents' notice afterwards. Why didn't the members of the public take it away with them?"

"That's the nasty bit. Inspector Matthews thinks they left it there so it could be used again."

"Nice photos, Ted," the Superintendent remarked.

"Taken by Mrs Grant's head gardener, on her instructions," said Matthews. "Make her twice as tall and put her in high heels and she'd do fine as a Detective-Inspector."

The Superintendent picked out two of the photographs. "You say these two have form?"

"They both used to be side-kicks for a villain called Jack de Courcy, that's his file in front of you. This one's Gordon Grimshaw who Mrs Grant and Co. say was an accessory after the fact in Robelin's murder. He used to be the gardener-handyman at a house de Courcy had in Maidenhead, drove the getaway car when he wasn't inside for grievous bodily harm. The other's his nephew, Martin Wates, got a record as long as your arm. The other gardeners may be clean. Records can't trace them."

The Superintendent opened the file. "Look here, Ted, you don't know de Courcy's behind this. He's supposed to have retired, gone to live in Spain."

"That's what it says in the file. But they get bored in Spain and they come back. Besides, it all fits. Have a look at his form."

The Superintendent ruffled through the file. "Summarize all

139

this for me, would you Ted?"

"Illegal exports of high-tech equipment to Bloc countries. Most of it stolen, often off trucks in transit. Some of the snatches were very violent. Back in the seventies we seem to have suspected that de Courcy had a contact in the Ministry who told him about gadgets on the embargo list that were worth stealing and flogging to the Soviets, and where to find them. There's also something in the file about dodgy export licences thought to have been provided by the same Ministry contact."

"Who was never found?"

"No. Lindsay was questioned, but so were a lot of others."

"And you're saying it was him all the time? A man who became Permanent Secretary and retired with a knighthood?"

"It's possible. I looked him up and he was at one of the right desks at the right time."

"'Possible' isn't good enough, Ted. You need to be damn sure."

"I've checked with Surrey CID. They confirm everything that Mrs Grant says about the goings-on at Monk's Mead, and they're sure Lindsay's hiding something, they've caught him out telling lies."

The Superintendent grunted sceptically and dived into the file. "Another thing, de Courcy's a bit old for a come-back, Ted, he's over seventy."

"He'd have to be, wouldn't he? Mrs Grant reckons he got his hooks into Lindsay back in 1941 over that Soviet Embassy business."

"Ted, you don't have to buy all her hunches."

"She has an embarrassing habit of being right, she is over this. It's in the file, how he started up as a kid, blackmailed two homosexual officials in the Ministry of Food and set himself up with a racket in blank ration books. He's not gay but he could pass as one, and that was how he operated, mixed with the gays at a club they all went to in Orange Street, then put the screws on them. Mrs Grant reckons the row between Lindsay and Mortlock was common knowledge among their friends. If de Courcy was moving in those circles he'd have heard about it."

140

The Superintendent brooded for a moment. "Okay then, go ahead but watch your step. What'll you do? Know where de Courcy's living, do we?"

"Not since he got back from Spain."

"Damn. Trace him through young Barton, can we?"

"I don't see how."

"Talk to his contacts. He was collecting information about Mortlock from people who'd known him. They'd pass him on from one to the other. Someone says 'you should talk to Jack de Courcy, he knew Mortlock.' De Courcy's being asked questions he doesn't like. Barton's put two and two together so he's for the chop."

"No. Sorry, Super, wrong scenario. No elderly gay friend of Lindsay's going to tell Barton 'you ought to interview a shady racketeer and blackmailer who's just back from Spain, and whose address I happen to have.'"

"Then what's the right scenario, Ted?"

"The elderly gay rings Lindsay, not de Courcy, and says 'I think I should warn you there's a young man going the rounds who knows far too much about you and Anthony Mortlock'. Lindsay passes the news on to de Courcy through the frighteners and says 'please do something about this'. De Courcy doesn't want Lindsay blown any more than Lindsay does, so Barton gets an invite to Sunningdale."

"Which is where de Courcy isn't, knowing him. What are Surrey doing about that? Enquiries at the station? Taxi drivers?"

"Yes, but that won't get them far. Somebody claiming to have reminiscences of Mortlock will have met Barton with a car and driven him God knows where on the pretext of a drink and a look at some manuscript poems he's got. We've one lead, though. Gordon Grimshaw — he's the head frightener at Monk's Mead — has a brother in Camberley with a garden maintenance business."

"So?"

"The business is a front for robbery with violence and Camberley's only three or four miles from Sunningdale. I've asked Surrey to concentrate on large unoccupied houses belonging to Arabs and such, there are maintenance firms that look after those places in the owner's absence. They've been asked to look out for anything unusual such as freshly dug earth in any of the gardens."

"No hope of Barton being alive?"

"No, de Courcy seems to be in a very savage mood. Look what he did to that Frenchman who happened along wanting a leak."

"Ted, we must get de Courcy this time."

"We can, him and Lindsay. Official Secrets Act, if this firm's working on secret government contracts. I'll report when I get back from there."

RGP Electronics was based in a seedy industrial estate off the North Circular Road. How low-profile can you get, Matthews asked himself as he drove through the gate into its potholed car park. Security was good, his identity had been checked efficiently by the gateman, who was watching to make sure he reported to reception and nowhere else. But the office block was unimpressive and the reception area carried the no-frills policy too far, even the plastic house plants needed dusting. The office of Roger George Patterson, founder, chairman and majority shareholder of the firm, was no better. Matthews found it hard to believe that the careworn man in shirt sleeves behind the battered desk was, on paper at least, a millionaire. One of the new-style 'grey' millionaires though, who had emerged in slump-ridden Britain; the ones with grim workaholic life styles who lived in ordinary houses, drove themselves to work in ordinary cars instead of flaunting a chauffeur-driven Rolls, and knew that if they had a heart attack the shares would plummet and they would stop being millionaires at once.

"We have reason to believe," Matthews began, "that an attempt will shortly be made to breach your firm's security."

Patterson stared at him with weary eyes in an unhealthy face. "What reason have you to believe any such thing?"

"I'd find it easier to explain if we could have a look at your

142

security arrangements first," said Matthews. It was too soon in the interview to come out with his shock accusation against a director of the firm.

"Right, I'll show you round," said Patterson.

Everything was as it should be securitywise. Photocopier under lock and key, tight stock control to prevent pilfering, a ban on unescorted visitors, a secure perimeter fence, night watchmen with guard dogs, staff identity badges worn all the time and colour coded to limit access to the drawing office and other restricted areas.

"That only leaves staff loyalty," Patterson summed up. "I think that's okay on the design and development side, though there's always the risk of someone learning all he can from us, then leaving and setting up on his own. But you're interested in the workforce I imagine."

"No, but go on about them," said Matthews.

"When we've developed a new product ahead of the competition, an underwater exploration gadget or whatever, we sub-contract the key components, each to a different sub-contractor. They don't know what the component's going into, and the workforce doesn't know the inner workings of the component. All we do here is an assembly job."

"Is anything with an Official Secrets classification going through at the moment? On a Defence Ministry contract, say?"

"No."

"Nothing that a competitor at the high-tech end of the armaments industry would be interested in?"

Patterson halted in his tracks. "Look, I'm not telling you any more till I know what this is about."

"I have reason to believe that one of your directors, Sir Julian Lindsay, is being blackmailed into supplying an interested party with information of the kind I've mentioned."

Patterson digested this. He was a little surprised, but not distressed. He had never warmed to Lindsay, he was a cold good-looking fish with no guts, hiring him had been a mistake. The firm's accountant had talked him into taking on someone with good government contacts, but Lindsay had the wrong kind of mind. The Civil Service fiddled gloomily with insoluble problems and hoped they would go away, or at best tried to prevent them becoming critical. In the private sector a problem was something that was there for management to solve. But not by people with minds like Lindsay's.

"Being blackmailed?" he echoed. "What is it, buggery?"

"That sort of thing, yes."

"Ah well, you have to take the smooth with the rough. I needed someone smooth to handle Whitehall, I can't stand all that wining and dining. He's not much use, hasn't brought in a single contract yet, and now he's taken himself off on holiday."

"Playing for time, most likely. Your trade secrets can't be blackmailed out of him when he's not here."

"Who's doing the blackmailing?" Patterson asked.

"An illicit arms dealer called De Courcy."

"Never heard of him, but I know what he'll be after. We've just gone into production with a new guidance system for the SS–7 guided missile."

Matthews frowned. "But isn't the SS–7 a Soviet weapon? Or am I wrong?"

"No, you're right. it's a bit confusing, no one knows this goes on, but the electronics are always a bit crude on the Soviet weaponry that they sell to the Third World, there's a gap in the market that we fill. A lot of Third World countries have bought the SS–7 and found it too hit-or-miss, we've contracts with three Middle East governments to upgrade it with a new guidance system."

"Why's de Courcy interested in that? What's in it for him?"

"The money the Russians would pay him for one of our systems to take apart and copy. If they could get it into production quick and peddle it round the Middle East they'd look a bit less silly."

"What would de Courcy want Lindsay to do?" Matthews asked. "Feed him technical information?"

"Hell no, Lindsay couldn't make head or tail of it, and you know where we keep the photocopier."

"De Courcy specializes in stealing high-tech stuff off trucks

144

when it's in transit. Could Lindsay help him there?"

"Oho," said Patterson thoughtfully. "That does ring a bell. I wasn't sure whether to believe you. Now I do."

"Explain, please."

"Lindsay's made two attempts to find out from me who the sub-contractors are who make the components, and what the arrangements are for delivering the components to us."

"But you didn't tell him?"

"Hell no, it's none of his business and I said so. The only people who know that are me and the production manager."

"How long ago was all this?"

"Back in May–June. Since then he's been taking a quiet interest in vehicles that come into the loading bay, I couldn't make out why."

Mrs Grant's got it right yet again, Matthews thought. Lindsay can't give de Courcy what he wants because he can't get the information. De Courcy thinks he's stalling, hence the dead cats and whatnot at Monk's Mead.

"When does Lindsay get back from leave?"

"Monday."

"How do the components get here from the sub-contractors?"

"Security van. A different firm for each sub-contractor. If you want to set a trap I'll cooperate."

It was an attractive idea, but uncomfortable. "The trouble is, your gadget's not on the British secret list, the know-how's only a trade secret. Industrial espionage isn't a criminal offence."

"Hell, man. You mean, I've got to let Lindsay do his stuff, then sue him for damages?"

"Technically, yes."

"Can't you stretch a point?"

"The trouble is, we'd be setting a police trap in a civil case, that's a bit dodgy. I'll have to consult my superiors and come back to you, okay?"

As Matthews drove back to the Yard a plan for trapping de Courcy took shape in his head. He was pleased with it, but when he outlined it to the Superintendent it went down badly.

"No, Ted. You'd be inciting de Courcy to commit a felony."

"He doesn't need any inciting, Super."

"Look, as long as he sticks to industrial spying he's Patterson's headache and nothing to do with us. You're asking permission to trap him into doing something that brings him into the net of the criminal law."

"Yes. Why not?"

"Because if it went wrong and got a lot of publicity, you'd have the civil liberties industry shouting its head off about *agents provocateurs* and morally grey areas."

"How could it go wrong?"

"By ending up with a shoot-out in the street complete with corpses, the public hates that and so do we."

"For Pete's sake Super, de Courcy's a dangerous maniac, look what he did to Robelin for no reason at all. We can't get him on that, he's covered his tracks too well. We must get him on something before he does any more damage."

There was a long silence. "Okay then Ted, but for God's sake be careful. What's that you've got there?"

Matthews handed him an application to the Home Secretary to tap Lindsay's phones at the London flat and at Monk's Mead.

"You're sure you need this? Can't you have him tailed instead?"

"He'll deal with de Courcy on the phone. Besides, a tail might scare him."

"The family down at Monk's Mead know we're on to him. That's what's going to frighten him off, one careless word would be enough."

"I've warned them, they'll watch it. The son's only adopted and hates his old man's guts. The girl's a bit of an unknown quantity, but she's not on speaking terms with him."

"What about Lady Lindsay?"

"She's more or less out of it having a nervous breakdown."

Mary Lindsay lay on her bed with her eyes shut. Julian stood over her holding out a cup of tea.

"Are you going to drink this or not?" he asked.

"In a minute. Put it down somewhere, for goodness' sake."

"Mary, there is nothing wrong with you except in your imagination. Pull yourself together and drink your tea."

She sat up and glared at him. "I shall drink it when I choose, and I want to ask you something. Why did you tell me the police had a theory that Robelin was murdered because of something that happened at . . . what was the place called? Oh yes, Bruay-en-Artois."

"I think they abandoned that theory in the end."

"They never held it, Julian."

"What on earth d'you mean?"

"What I say, it was never a police theory. One of them told me the other day that it was only a suggestion of yours, that they agreed to look into."

"Oh nonsense. You weren't concentrating, you don't seem capable of it nowadays. You must have misunderstood."

"I understood perfectly. I made him repeat it to make sure."

"Then it must have been a different policeman from the one who mentioned the Bruay business to me. Mary, we open to the public in ten minutes. My holiday, so called, though it has hardly been restful, ends tomorrow and I shall no longer be available to do your job for you, so you'll have to stop lolling on your bed and take charge in the garden. Why not start pulling yourself together now?"

"I'll be down in a minute, Julian."

"No, now."

"Oh very well . . . ." She swung her feet off the bed on to the floor and felt for her shoes. She had no headache, just a weary feeling that there was something unbearably heavy inside her skull. Her mind was clear enough to know that Julian had lied, but not clear enough to work out why he needed to lie about anything as serious as murder.

"Monk's Mead, Julian Lindsay speaking."

"Good morning, Kitty dear, how are you?"

"I told you not to phone me here and don't call me 'Kitty', it isn't funny."

"But Kitty, I keep telling you, you mustn't squirm whenever I hint at your gay and goatish past, it's bad for your mental health. Back to work tomorrow, eh? Did you enjoy your holiday?"

"No."

"Oh what a pity, I did hope you'd return to your electronic grindstone refreshed and ready for a real effort. Because Kitty, I must talk to you very seriously for your own good. I'm disappointed with you, you must try harder, your results simply aren't good enough."

"I've explained to you over and over again, there's no way I can get you what you call 'the results'."

"But there must be a way, it's just a matter of making that little extra effort. It's this British disease of defeatism, you just haven't got the will to win, what's happened? You used to be one of my most productive helpers."

"In quite different and more favourable circumstances."

"I don't understand, you're a director of the firm. Surely you're entitled to know?"

"Apparently not, and if I did get what you want out of them and tell you, they'd know at once who had tipped you off. I wish you'd get this into your head, there's no way I can get you the information you want without the leak being traced back to me."

"Who cares if it is, Kitty love? I don't."

"Perhaps not, but I do."

"Oh dear, this is the moment of truth. If there's one thing I hate, it's having to tell someone it's time for them to retire. You've been useful to me over the years, but there's only one more thing I want that you can give me, and you're expendable when I've got it."

"Well, you're not going to get it, so for God's sake stop behaving like Frankenstein's monster. I'm sick of you mucking me about."

"Don't you dare talk to me like that, you raddled old closet queer. Do what you're bloody told or you'll wish you'd never been born."

"Do try to control yourself and stop talking nonsense."

"You're making me angry. I'm going to have one of my headaches, I feel it coming on. You know what happens when I get angry and have a headache."

"Yes, but it won't happen to me. Unless you stop this Mad Hatter act of

*yours at once, I shall disappear, apparently suffering from loss of memory,
and I shan't reappear till Patterson has cleaned up the Middle East
market and the thing you're hoping to steal from him isn't worth its weight
in second-hand silicon chips."*

*"You shit. You slimy senile bugger. Listen, I want that information by
next Sunday, and if I don't fucking get it by then I'll see you damn well do
disappear. And when you turn up again at Monk's Mead you'll find the
police wondering who sent your wife the photos of you hard at it with that
pretty young soldier you used to fancy, and why someone cut your poor
Mary to bits with your wood axe, and why you haven't got an alibi. Now
get up off your sodomized arse and let's have some action."*

As usual on a Monday morning Patterson was in his office
before eight to start acting on the decisions he had reached in a
weekend of sombre brooding at home. He liked to clear his desk
before the phone began to ring, but today his luck was out.
Inspector Matthews was on the line, sounding worried.

"Can we put the operation forward a week? It's become
much more urgent."

"Yes, except that what he wants will be falling plop in his lap
the moment he's back from holiday. Won't he smell a rat?"

"No, he's in a desperate fix. He wouldn't smell a decaying
elephant."

"What's the hurry?" Patterson asked.

"Some fresh information's just come in. De Courcy's making
death threats against Lindsay's wife unless he delivers the
goods quick."

"You have good sources. Phone tap?"

"No comment. De Courcy's quite capable of it, we need to get
moving before anything nasty happens."

"Right. This Thursday instead of next?"

"Does that give them time to take the bait and get
organized?"

"They're probably all set already for when they get the tip-
off."

They had already agreed how the trap was to be baited.
Patterson slipped a carbon into a memo pad and wrote on it,

then crumpled the top copy in his pocket to be destroyed later. He slipped the carbon copy into an envelope and sealed it, then considered the next question: Who?

Hodgson, the head of the dispatch room? He was a steady old buffer, he could be relied on to keep his mouth shut but not, repeat not, to put on an amateur theatrical performance that would convince Lindsay. He would be dire, and so too in their different way would any of the girls who worked under him, excitable creatures who would over-act grossly. But there was also a nice sensible middle-aged woman, a Mrs Dixon who worked part time. He sent for her and briefed her, then handed her the sealed envelope.

"Now, Mrs Dixon, let's make quite sure we've got this straight. When my secretary sends for you, you come in here and you give me the envelope, and what do you say?"

She repeated it word for word.

"Fine, Mrs Dixon. And don't tell anyone, before or after. Not even your husband, till I tell you you may."

"Yes, Mr Patterson, I quite understand."

Amazing, thought Patterson. How can a man in such a God-awful mess look as relaxed as that?

Lindsay, summoned for a briefing after his holiday, had just sauntered into the office, impeccably dressed as usual and ready to settle down for what, if he had his way, would be a time-wasting exchange of gossip. He must be living at one remove from reality, Patterson thought as he made conversation about a tender for underwater tracking equipment on a torpedo practice range. What kind of person was hiding behind the imposing, meaningless presence? Was there anyone there at all?

After what seemed a long time but was probably about right, the secretary buzzed to announce someone from the dispatch room with an urgent message. Mrs Dixon was shown in clutching the envelope, with just the right degree of anxiety on her placid face.

"I'm sorry to interrupt, Mr Patterson, but Mr Hodgson sent me with this, he says you ought to see it at once."

150

Patterson opened the envelope and took out the sheet from the memo pad.

"My God!" he cried on a note of would-be panic. "Where did Mr Hodgson find this?"

He had over-acted grossly. It sounded phoney even to him.

"It was on the floor of the dispatch room when we came in this morning," said the admirable Mrs Dixon calmly. "Mr Hodgson found it and put it in the envelope and told me to bring it to you."

"You mean, it's been lying about in there since before the weekend?" he cried, sounding even less genuine than before.

"I don't know, Mr Patterson. Mr Hodgson didn't say."

When she had gone Patterson took a grip on himself, and managed to tone down the drama as he said: "This is a shocker, it's the job docket for one of the security firms that collect from the sub-contractors."

"Does it matter?" Lindsay asked languidly.

"It matters the hell of a lot. Every Thursday when they deliver, I give the driver the instructions for the following week's run." He rummaged in a desk drawer. "It's the carbon copy, I keep those in here and the one for this week's missing. Damn. I must have given the driver both copies by mistake, and he dropped the carbon in the dispatch room."

"I suppose that is unfortunate," Lindsay murmured.

"It damn well is, take a look at it."

This was the tricky part. Normally a different security firm would collect from each of the sub-contractors. This time, exceptionally, all the eggs would be in one basket. According to the docket one van would be collecting from all four sub-contractors, so that in two days' time anyone holding it up would be able to grab all the components of an improved, secret guidance system for an SS–7 anti-aircraft missile. Would Lindsay sniff the tempting bait, decide that it was too good to be true, and fight shy of entering the trap? Patterson talked on about how one of their usual security firms had gone broke, another had raised its charges exorbitantly and a third was having staffing problems, leaving only one to do all the runs.

"So I decided to risk it for once," he explained. "But now I'm not sure. That docket's been lying about in the dispatch room since last Thursday for any Tom, Dick or Harry to see."

He had been watching Lindsay's face as he spoke. It was amazing, here was the man's chance to get his blackmailer off his back with the suspicion spread all round the factory, but his expression betrayed nothing, he was as cold and nerveless as a reptile.

"I'm worried, d'you think I should cancel the run?" Patterson asked.

"Oh, is that really necessary?" Lindsay murmured without sounding specially interested. "I know security's important, but can't you chance it for once?"

"I'll talk to the production manager, see how urgently he needs the components," said Patterson. Leaving the docket on his desk, he darted out of the office and chatted to the production manager for two minutes by his watch, long enough for Lindsay to absorb the information left temptingly to hand. When he went back the job docket was exactly where he had left it and Lindsay was deeply absorbed in the technical specification of the torpedo range equipment, which he could not conceivably have understood.

"They need the parts this week," Patterson told him. "I daren't postpone the run, we'll have to risk it."

Lindsay smiled at him, rather oddly. His hands were shaking a little. It was the first glimpse Patterson had seen of the man behind the cold, polite façade.

Lindsay was struggling desperately to control his excitement. Here, handed out on a plate, was the information that de Courcy wanted. It had been lying around for days in the dispatch room for anyone to get hold of, there would be no way of proving that the leak came from him. He might be suspected, but if the worst came to the worst there was a way of dealing with that, he had seen in a flash how to turn this wonderful windfall to his advantage.

One phase of his battle of wits with de Courcy was over. Quite a new war game was about to begin.

NINE

"*Good morning, how are you today?*"

"*Oh, it's you, Kitty, what can I do for you?*"

"*I'm making you an offer.*"

"*Good, you've changed your mind. Let's hear.*"

"*The name of the security firm. The registration number of the van. The names and addresses of the sub-contractors where it will call to pick up the components, the date and approximate time of arrival at our plant with all the components on board. My price for this information is five hundred thousand pounds.*"

"*Kitty, your mind must have given way. Or else you are drunk.*"

"*On the contrary, I'm simply making prudent provision for my declining years. As I told you, I shall have to disappear abroad before the leak is traced to me, and I intend to have a comfortable exile.*"

"*But Kitty, you don't understand. I want the information but I don't want to give you all that money. So why don't I send some friends of mine round to your place for a little chat?*"

"*Because they won't find me there. I'm at a pay phone now and I shan't be anywhere where you can find me until my bank in Lausanne confirms that the money's been paid in. When they've confirmed, you shall have the information.*"

"*Oh dear, this offer of yours doesn't sound to me at all attractive. Let's forget about it and I'll go on making your life miserable until you change your mind.*"

"*Ah, but I shan't change my mind and the offer is unrepeatable.*"

"*I'll have your balls off before I give you a penny.*"

"*How unpleasant, but you'll have to catch me first.*"

"*Kitty, I warn you. You're making me cross again.*"

"*I daresay, but if you want to do a deal you must decide quickly. The time-scale for making your arrangements is very short.*"

"There's no problem, we can make this a dummy run. I'd like to see how reliable your information is, and a rehearsal is always a wise precaution. Then we can make our plans for the next run at greater leisure."

"I'm afraid that's not possible."

"Oh, but why not?"

"Because there won't be another opportunity like this, not for months anyway. Normally there's a separate run for each sub-contractor, you'd have to attack four different vans to get a complete set of the components. This time there's a crisis, they're sending one van round to collect the lot. That's why the offer's unrepeatable."

"But Kitty, how do I know you're not telling me a pack of lies?"

"You don't, you have to take a chance. I'll ring you back at two to find out what you've decided. Don't try to beat me down, by the way. I rather fancy Switzerland for my exile, and living there's expensive."

At the Watford Gap service area on the motorway, Julian Lindsay put down the pay phone in a glow of satisfaction. De Courcy would have to part with the money, he had no choice. He would hate shelling out half a million and would use crude strong-arm methods to try to get it back. But that could be dealt with easily, by disappearing abroad without trace. Not to Switzerland of course, he had thrown that in to mislead. Somewhere with a good climate and obliging oriental house-boys . . . .

The prospect was attractive. His wife was a neurotic bore and his son loathed him, he would have made the break long ago but for lack of money. He had had to pour every spare penny into the bottomless pit of the Monk's Mead garden, because if he didn't old Mrs Mortlock's lawyers would unseal the envelope that she had lodged with them and reveal its embarrassing contents to the world.

But he had no intention of fleeing the country in a hurry. That would be to admit his guilt, lose his Civil Service pension, be stripped of his knighthood. He would make his departure from the scene a gradual process. He would probably be suspected of being de Courcy's informant but nothing could be proved and it was not a crime to go and live abroad. There

154

would be no pretext for taking away his pension, which would be needed to keep Mrs Mortlock's lawyers quiet and the Monk's Mead garden afloat. Nowadays half a million was not a lot, and de Courcy might beat him down.

De Courcy was the danger. He would be furious when he discovered that he had paid over huge sums to a fugitive-to-be who had not fled. But there was a neat way of dealing with that, he had drafted the letter already in his head.

My dear Patterson,

As I told you in my phone call before the weekend, my wife's mental condition is very much more serious than I had realized. Acting on medical advice I have taken her to a clinic here in Vienna where she has had treatment before. She is still in a very disturbed state, and I am afraid I shall have to stay here with her for the present.

I shall probably need to devote myself to my dear wife's health for some time to come, and have been considering my future with the company. It has been a disappointment to me, and I think also to you, to find that my performance in what is to me the very unfamiliar field of private industry has not been as effective as we had both hoped. I am therefore writing to tender my resignation. . . .

He would not return to England. While they were in Vienna he would reach an understanding with Mary about their separation, she would be delighted to see the last of him. Adam could come out there to escort her home, and as far as de Courcy knew, Julian Lindsay would have "fled abroad".

"Hullo there. Are you taking up my unrepeatable offer?"

"Well Kitty, I thought I might manage a small gratuity if everything turns out well."

"I shall ignore that irrelevant remark and assume that the answer to my question is 'no'."

"My God, Kitty, you've got a nerve."

"If I may say so, so have you. You've undertaken to deliver something

155

you haven't got to a customer who's in a hurry, and you're in danger of losing face by falling down on the delivery date. In your position I wouldn't try to wriggle out of paying the rate for the job. I object strongly, by the way to being addressed as 'Kitty', it's very offensive."

"But you'll have to put up with that, won't you, Kitty?"

"No, I shall hang up on you now as a punishment, to teach you manners. I'll ring again in an hour and hope to find you more reasonable. But as I say, the timetable for making your arrangements is very tight, and you've just cut it by an hour by being rude. Goodbye for now."

"Wait, Julian. Hullo? . . . Hullo?"

Inspector Matthews stared at the map. Where would the attack come? After the van had collected from all four sub-contractors, till then there would be no point. That meant after its call at the last of them, Buckhurst Pressings Limited of Chingford. From there on it would be at risk for twelve miles, all the way along the North Circular Road, till it turned off into the industrial estate in Hanger Lane, to deliver its load at RGP Electronics. He won't try anything after that, Matthews reasoned, because the estate's a mass of dead ends, they'd be in trouble with their getaway. He'd be a fool if he tried to mount a hold-up on the fast double-track sections of the North Circular, but there's a dodgy bit with traffic lights round Barnet, or his best bet might be when the van leaves the factory at Chingford, before it gets into the fast traffic. . . .

But Records say that on past form he's a bloodthirsty psychopath, can one rely on him not to do anything crazy?

No, Matthews decided, and began staring at the map all over again.

"Here we are again, and please remember not to call me by that offensive name. Well? What have you decided?"

"Two hundred thousand. Half now, half later."

"How ridiculous. I think we'd better forget the whole idea, you're obviously not in a businesslike mood."

"Well, what's your figure?"

"I told you. Half a million."

"No. That's more than the job's worth. A quarter."

"I might consider four hundred thousand."

"No. Two fifty, half now, half afterwards. That's my highest."

"Unfortunately, 'half afterwards' is open to the objection that it might not materialize."

"But 'all now' is open to the objection that you might tiptoe off to the continent tomorrow with it, leaving your fellow-directors perplexed and me without a van to hijack."

"Then we're back at five hundred thousand."

"Four."

"No. Five, if you're splitting it."

". . . Okay then, I'll meet your figure, but on one condition. You stop this darting about among the pay phones and turn up at your office all present and correct by Thursday at latest and put on a convincing show of business as usual to impress me and your fellow directors with your honest behaviour."

"Very well then, that's settled. You have the number of my Swiss account, and you've time to make the transfer before the banks there close. I'll ring them in the morning, and if the money's there you shall the information you want. Okay?"

"Okay then, okay."

"And about the other half. In case you were thinking of not paying your debts in full, do remember that I know a great deal about you that would interest the authorities in several countries, and that when my shocking behaviour has been made public there will be very little harm any talkativeness by you can do me."

"My God, Kitty, which of us is blackmailing who?"

Several people did not sleep easily that night. De Courcy lay awake thinking of ways to get his money back from Lindsay. Inspector Matthews, tossing and turning beside his wife in their double bed at Ealing, had visions of the security van being held up on a fast section of the North Circular Road, with following vehicles crashing into it in a multiple pile-up. Tessa dreamed that Peter Barton was dead but came back from the grave and tried to make love to her, a thing he had attempted clumsily shortly before he was kidnapped. Mary Lindsay dreamed in horror of her mother's dying moments, and Adam dreamed of killing Lindsay to free all concerned from the fossilized garden to which they were enslaved. Celia had a repeat of her standard nightmare, to the effect that she was a saxifrage and pot-bound, with her roots squeezed agonizingly in a too-small pot. This was a dream she had when she was under tension. Why was she having it now, she wondered in the morning. The tension was over, she had unloaded the Monk's Mead problem on to the police and could forget it.

Only Julian Lindsay slept peacefully in the motel near Birmingham where he had gone to ground. He had the precious gift of not worrying once the decisions had been taken for better or worse. Without that knack, he could never have survived the life he had had to lead since he walked into the Soviet Embassy in London in the autumn of 1941.

"Good morning. I've rung the bank and everything seems to be in order for Thursday – "

"Thursday! Hell, Kitty, that gives us very little time."

"It's your fault for havering, and don't call me Kitty. Have you a pencil to take this down? The van comes from North London Security Services, registration number A447 LMO, and it's painted dark green with the firm's name on the side. The first pick-up point is at the Basildon firm that makes the laser heads at about eight on Thursday morning. . . ."

"Inspector Matthews? Surrey CID here. We think we've found Barton's body."

"Congratulations. How did you manage that?"

"Your hunch was right, there's a big property in a wood between Sunningdale and Camberley, belongs to Mick McLattery who's the star of a pop group called Mindless Violence — "

"Good heavens!"

"Well yes, we get all sorts here. They're away touring the States and the house is empty. The maintenance firm sent a man to clear out the roof gutters and while he was up his ladder he noticed faint tyre marks going across the main lawn and he reported it. That was a bit of luck, you'd never have spotted them from the ground. We investigated and found a place in

158

the far corner of the garden where fresh turf had been laid, as if to repair a worn patch. The maintenance firm hadn't arranged to have that done and the neighbours said that a van similar to the one used by the Grimshaw firm had been seen in the area. So we sent for the spades and there he was under the turf."

"Well done. You're sure it's him?"

"He corresponds to the description, so we've asked Miss Lindsay to come and make a positive identification."

"Oh . . . why not his parents?"

"They're abroad on holiday, address unknown."

"I see . . . ."

"Miss Lindsay was the obvious person, seeing that she first reported him missing, she's on her way here now. I hope we haven't done the wrong thing?"

"No. No, I think that's okay. Have you told the media?"

"No."

"Well don't, and if they ask say we're anxious that nothing should be published till after Thursday."

Tessa hurried back to Monk's Mead along the lane from the bus stop. Cold shivers ran up and down her back. The policeman at the mortuary in Camberley had been kind, but seeing a dead person for the first time in her life had made her turn queer and vomit.

Poor Peter. She had cried at the mortuary, but with tears of anger. Dying was for old people, not for him, he was pompous and skinny, but he would have got over that in time. It was disgraceful, fancy killing someone to keep a forty-year-old secret. There ought to be no secrets, they caused most of the world's troubles. When she was through with university she would be a journalist, the investigative kind, she would pry and pry, nothing would be secret if she could help it.

It was well after twelve. She should have reported for duty in the kitchen half an hour ago, and there looking daggers at her from the entrance to the tea-barn like Lady Macbeth was Gran, waiting to put the boot in because she was late.

As she went past, Gran gripped her arm and said "Tessa!"

159

"Let go of me, Gran, I couldn't help it," said Tessa, shaking herself free.

"What? What?" shouted Gran with a wild gesture.

The angry tears had started again. Tessa blinked them back. "Your pet hate's dead," she blurted out. "Peter Barton's been murdered. The police made me go and identify him, that's why I'm late."

She might as well not have spoken, Gran seemed not to have heard. "I've lost my keys, Tessa," she said jerkily. "The whole damn bunch, aren't I a fool? You haven't seen them?"

"No, Gran."

"I must have dropped them in the garden, any of those vulgar nuisances in there could have picked them up and walked into the house. It's a disaster, Julian will half kill me, what am I to do?"

Tessa saw dimly through her own misery that Gran was in a very agitated state. It was absurd to get so worked up about a bunch of keys, but Gran's misery touched a chord in her. "I'll come and help you find them, Gran."

"Oh no, Tessa dear. One must stand on one's own feet, one mustn't be a nuisance. I must pull myself together and find them myself." She turned to go, then paused. "Did you say someone was dead?"

It's got through at last, thought Tessa. Speaking very slowly and distinctly she said: "Peter Barton's dead. It's awful. He was killed because he knew too much about Great-Uncle Anthony, what d'you think of that?"

Surely Gran would react now, ask questions, comfort her a little, help her to forget that ordeal in the mortuary. But no, Gran's hands made a fluttering gesture of rejection, as if Peter's death was altogether too much, an event that could not be coped with. She turned away without a word, leaving Tessa standing there.

Only then did Tessa remember. The police had told her not to mention anything about the case to anyone at Monk's Mead.

Mary Lindsay hurried back through the crowd of visitors in the Long Borders towards the house. I am in a bad way, she told herself, the way I am in is very bad, but I must remember not to scream and make faces at these idiotic people. So that wretched boy is dead, is he? I ought to be glad but I'm not. He sniffed around like some horrid little dog and found out that darling Anthony was a traitor, but now he is dead and the shocking secret we have kept for so long is safe, so why am I not cock-a-hoop?

Because I never cared for blood sports, that's it.

Julian has gone too far, killing that wretched boy and the Frenchman before that. Well if he didn't kill the Frenchman answer me this: why did he tell that fib about wherever-it-was, that village in France? Anyway, how had the Frenchman found out about Anthony, and what damn business was it of his? He must have found out, otherwise Julian wouldn't have wanted to kill him.

How odd. Why did this never occur to me before? Because I'm going batty, I suppose, but now I come to think of it I don't care how many people know that Anthony was a traitor. He was a beast, he pulled my hair and broke my dolls and he was spoilt because he was handsome and I wasn't, and I hated him. Julian has always been much keener on keeping the secret than I am. When he first told me what Anthony had done, he insisted that we must keep it from Mother at all costs because she doted so on Anthony. And we did, but in the end it was a waste of effort, it turned out she'd known all along, what a hoot! Just before she died, when she was going a bit mad with the pain, she blabbed it all out. Got it a bit wrong though, she thought Julian was the traitor. But that was absurd, Julian didn't work at Bletchley so how could he have given away Bletchley secrets to the Russians? She was very confused by then, talked nonsense about everything.

Julian *enjoys* killing people, that must be it. But how dare he organize silly pompous Barbara into sneaking out of her conference in Brighton and giving Mother those pills, if he'd asked me first I'd never have agreed. That woman at the inquest was right, mercy killing *is* wrong. I should have stood up when Barbara was giving evidence and shouted 'look at her, look at that lady with the tidy hair who sits on Royal Commissions, she's lying, she's a murderess.' That's why I'm being punished, for not speaking out. I am guilty, my garden is being wrecked because I didn't tell everyone what Barbara is really like.

Julian terrifies me. So does Barbara. They whisper about me behind my back, I suppose she was his mistress once. Mother said something about Adam not being Anthony's son, but that was just her deathbed nonsense, he certainly isn't Julian's. It's too disgusting, the idea of those two heaving and sweating and grunting and engendering darling Adam. No, I won't think about it, it's not true.

Julian is wicked, it's his fault that I'm in a bad way. He is much worse than Anthony who only broke my dolls and pulled my hair and then got killed. Julian didn't get killed, he went on and on at me, nag nag nag. Mother got it right after all. *Julian is the traitor who betrays life because he enjoys killing people.*

I am a hopeless incompetent. I ought to have weeded the Grey and Pink Garden this morning, and here I am stuck like an image in front of a locked door that I can't get through because I've lost my keys. I could weep with terror and despair.

"Mother, you're crying," said Adam's voice behind her. "What's the trouble?"

"Oh, Adam darling, thank goodness you've come. I can't cope any more and I hate this garden and if I see another rose that needs dead-heading I shall scream, and I can't get through this damn door because I've lost my keys."

"No you haven't. Here they are, in the pocket of your dress."

"Oh, so they are, how stupid of me."

"Cheer up, there's nothing to cry about."

"There is, Adam, how can you say that? Look at me, I'm quaking with terror. I've just found out that your father's a traitor and he's going to kill me."

So that's that, Celia thought with relief as she and Bill scuttled round the glass-houses catching up with arrears of work. Trapping Lindsay and his blackmailing arms dealer was

Scotland Yard's headache. She and Bill could get on with the real business of life, such as growing from seed a charming little scented cyclamen, quite hardy, which was in short supply because the population of the Lebanon had more important things to do than digging up the corms of *C.libanoticum* on the hills where it grew wild and exporting them to Europe.

The outside bell of the office telephone clanged and Bill, who was nearer, answered it.

"Adam Lindsay for you," he reported. "Now Celia, you just got them Lindsay nits out of your hair, don't let them jump in there again."

Adam sounded unnerved, his voice was trembling. His mother, it seemed, was now having the nervous breakdown that had threatened ever since the inquest on Mrs Mortlock. "And she's worked it out somehow that Dad's a 'traitor' as she puts it. She thinks he wants to murder her. She won't eat anything and she's been locked in her bedroom, phoning people."

"Who?" Celia asked. "I hope you listened on the downstairs phone?"

"She rang Dad's office. He wasn't there, but she talked a lot of nonsense to the secretary. Then she rang someone else, but there was no reply."

"Leave the phone off downstairs, that'll put a stop to it."

"Oh, I hadn't thought of that. Mrs Grant, you couldn't possibly come over? She's been wandering round the house half undressed, I can't do anything with her, I get too upset and that upsets her. A woman might find it easier to get through to her."

"I'll come straight over," said Celia.

So they found young Barton, de Courcy brooded, and dug him up. Fuck them.

I'm a fool. I should have had him put under the turf further away. I should have smashed his face in so he couldn't be recognized, taken a sledge-hammer to his teeth because of the damn dental records. Damn, I should have seen to all that, I've been careless, I'm a fool.

If the police find out who he is I'll be in the bloody *gazpacho*

163

and no mistake. It's the gossip of all the Sunningdale super-markets, why isn't there anything in the papers about it? Because the police know something and want to spring a surprise, that's why.

Fuck Mr Peter virgin-faced Barton. You could too if you were that way inclined, I bet he's one of those. Like Lindsay. They're filthy. No loyalties and no guts. Tony Mortlock was another, silly little fairy.

Why in Sodom's name did Barton have to do a lot of nosy research and write a damn thesis about Mortlock? It was amazing how some people got a mysterious satisfaction out of knowing things that weren't a damn bit of use, couldn't be turned into money or used as leverage. If you were plain Frederick Cooper and left school in Bermondsey at fourteen to earn ten bob a week as an errand boy, and if you wanted to get to the top of the pile and invent a grand name for yourself like Jack de Courcy, you had to concentrate on knowledge you could turn to use. And English grammar, of course, he'd sweated away at that. If you didn't talk grammar people would spot that de Courcy wasn't your real name and you didn't belong at the top of the pile.

Damn Barton, why did he want to go round asking all those paralytic old queers about a fifty-year-old scandal that didn't matter a fourpenny fuck to anyone except me and Julian Lindsay? Damn Lindsay too, think of him getting all that money.

My money, de Courcy thought, clenching his fists furiously. Eating into my profit margin, I was mad to let him have it and I was mad not to tidy up properly after the Barton business. I'm a fool, I've made a shocking mess of this whole thing. If it goes wrong I won't be safe in Spain, there's an extradition treaty now. Why the hell did I start it?

Be honest with yourself, Frederick Cooper. You started it because you were playing poker with the bullion robbery crowd, and they caught you cheating and made you look small and feel unsure of yourself and you wanted to prove to yourself that you were still the tops. But you aren't, you've lost your touch, you've let Lindsay string you along for months and then outsmart you, and now you're making silly mistakes. You're not the tops, you're past it.

"Mrs Grant?"

"Yes."

"Matthews here. Are you alone or is Lady Lindsay with you in the room?"

"Yes, I'm alone and no, I've got her to lie down upstairs. How did you know I was here?"

"I rang your home number and they told me you were at Monk's Mead. There's been a worrying development that you should know about. Lindsay seems to have gone into hiding."

"How odd, Inspector. Could he have taken fright for some reason?"

"We don't know what to make of it. He left his office yesterday at twelve, saying he had appointments in the afternoon and wouldn't be back. He didn't sleep at his London flat and this morning he rang his secretary saying he was off to Aberdeen to talk to some oil people. But we've checked with them, they're not expecting him till next week."

"But he's keeping in touch with his office and behaving as if nothing was wrong?"

"That's right. We don't know what he's playing at, but if he turns up at Monk's Mead, would you manage somehow to let us know at once?"

"Of course."

"How is Lady Lindsay? I'm told she rang her husband's secretary and talked very wildly, but I'm not sure what about."

"She isn't making much sense, but as far as I can make out she thinks her husband murdered Peter Barton."

"Really? How did she find out that Barton's dead?"

"Tessa, who doesn't believe in suppressing awkward truths, blurted it out. Lady Lindsay put two and two together at once and concluded that her husband had killed Barton."

"She could be right, Mrs Grant."

"Oh no, out of the question."

"Why not? She could have found out something we don't know."

"No really, Inspector. She's having a nervous breakdown, they often invent murderous fantasies about their husbands, it doesn't mean a thing.

Besides, he's not the murdering type."

"That's just hunch, you could be wrong. If Lindsay's jumpy already and she comes out with that, he could take fright and wreck this whole operation."

"Well, we must hope he doesn't turn up at Monk's Mead till it's all over."

De Courcy had got his balance back, he could breathe easily again. How absurd to have talked oneself into a panic about nothing. Peter Barton was buried four miles away, on the other side of the motorway. Even if the police discovered who he was, there was no way they could connect him with a retired businessman from the north, known by a name other than de Courcy, who had taken a furnished house in Sunningdale but would be safely back in Spain for good the day after tomorrow.

Why had he panicked? He distrusted and despised psychiatrists, who earned their living by inventing excuses for people who hadn't the guts to pull themselves together when they were down in the dumps. But he knew the psychiatrists' jargon and what label they would attach to him if they knew the way his mind see-sawed between his Highs and his Lows, as he called them. He hated the Lows, they belonged to a personality he despised and didn't recognize as his own, but he knew how to snap out of them. One had to pull off something really smart, something to prove that one was still at the top of the pile. And if people got hurt in the process, to hell with them.

He was through the Low now, it had proved to be quite a short one and he was feeling good. Everything was ready for the attack on the security van, and he had to laugh at the way he'd worked himself up into a paddy about the money Lindsay had had off him.

There was a simple way of getting it all back; quick, sure-fire, and possessing the essential element of complete surprise. Lindsay wouldn't know what had hit him till it was all over.

After two hours of hectic struggle with the situation at Monk's Mead, Celia had decided that she was not doing as well as could be expected. Mary Lindsay had refused either to finish undressing and get into bed or to dress completely, and had to be dissuaded from making sorties among the visitors in the garden in an intermediate state of disarray. Adam had been no help at all. He was busy with a crisis in the garden because two of the gardeners (Celia could guess which) had not reported for duty. The family doctor had taken far too long coming, and departed five minutes later leaving Celia to administer somehow the massive dose of sedative that Mary flatly refused to swallow. The next item on Julian's programme, she maintained, was to murder her, and she must remain alert to prevent it.

When the flaws in this reasoning had been pointed out to her several times, she had agreed to take an aspirin and lie down on her bed, and Celia was able to come downstairs and celebrate this triumph by helping herself ruthlessly to Julian's whisky. But she had barely taken one restorative sip when the telephone rang and she found herself having to soothe a perplexed and nervous Inspector Matthews.

"If he does turn up at Monk's Mead," Matthews had concluded, "I'm sure we can rely on you to keep him in play till we get there, and minimize the damage."

And how the hell am I supposed to do that, Celia asked herself crossly as she swigged at her whisky. No answer had occurred to her when the door of the living room opened unceremoniously and in walked Barbara Seymour.

"Oh. So you're here, Mrs Grant. How is she?"

"Having a nervous breakdown."

Barbara nodded. "Julian phoned me. He rang his secretary at the office and she told him."

"I see."

"How kind of you to step into the breach. I can take over now."

This proposal was objectionable for two reasons. First, Barbara was obviously under instructions to investigate the situation and report her findings to Julian, and this would unsettle Inspector Matthews. Secondly and more serious, an invasion of the sick room by Barbara would unsettle Mary, who was under the illusion that Barbara was Julian's mistress and a party to his plan to murder her.

"Thank you for offering, but it might not be a good idea," said Celia mildly. "She seems to have taken an irrational dislike to you as well as to Julian."

"Oh dear, I'd better talk to her. She's quite fond of me really, I can probably make her see reason."

She moved towards the stairs, but Celia was too quick for her. "Please. I've just persuaded her to take an aspirin and lie down."

Barbara glared at her like a frustrated bull. "Does what she's saying make any sense at all?"

"No."

Barbara looked relieved, but showed no signs of going. "I've always suspected that underneath, she was a bit jealous of my friendship with Julian. She probably feels she's not up to our weight intellectually. Has there been any trace of that?"

"Yes. And now if you'll excuse me, I think you'd better leave me to cope."

"Who's that down there?" called Mary's voice from above.

"Now look what you've done," Celia snapped. "Please go before she sees you."

Barbara did not move. Moments later, Mary appeared in the doorway in her dressing gown. "It's you, Barbara. I thought so. Get out."

Celia rounded on Barbara. "It took me hours to get her to bed," she muttered, "and now I'll have to start all over again."

"Get out, you self-important hypocrite," yelled Mary, enjoying herself hugely. "Get you to a nunnery go, shoo, bugger off."

"You hear?" snapped Celia. Emboldened by whisky and bad temper she added: "Go away and infest the corridors of power like the other busybodies, on the human level you're a disaster."

What a little spitfire, Barbara thought as she drove away, furious at being thrown out of the house by an intellectual inferior half her size, and with a surprisingly sharp tongue.

168

Moreover the harmless-looking Mrs Grant had blocked all her attempts to enquire into Mary Lindsay's state of mind. She would have nothing concrete to report to Julian.

Barbara was as worried as Julian by the possibility that all the skeletons were about to start falling out of their cupboards. A woman in her position could not afford to be laughed at. It was rather creditable to have had a stormy emotional past which included bearing the illegitimate child of a dead war-poet. She had quietly encouraged the gossip about her relationship with Anthony Mortlock, because it proved that one had experienced the human passions which one laid down the law about in one's public work. To be denounced as having invented a fictitious stormy past for oneself and publicized it was a different matter. She would be the laughing-stock of Whitehall, even if no one discovered that the illegit had resulted from a few furtive couplings with her landlady's handsome son in wartime Blackpool.

Exposure had threatened once already, when old Mrs Mortlock in her agony started blurting out the truths she had held back for so long. Fortunately they were too bizarre to be easily believed, and her jumbled utterances about them could be passed off to the doctor, the district nurse and others as the senile ramblings of extreme old age. Even Mary had failed to take them seriously. Quick action had scotched the danger, but she and Julian had not foreseen that people who disapproved of mercy killing would take it out on Mary by wrecking her garden. That had put Mary under strain, it was astonishing that the nervous breakdown had held off for so long.

Julian seemed to think that some fresh discovery had touched it off. More probably Mrs Mortlock's alleged ramblings had suddenly fitted together in her mind and made sense. In either case the situation would be very dangerous. Mary would blurt out the truth to everyone; her doctor, interfering little Mrs Grant, Adam, Tessa. It would be all round the neighbourhood in no time, and Tessa was one of those open-government maniacs who believed that no linen was too dirty to exhibit in public. She would make sure the whole embarrassing story got into the press.

But how much did Mary really know? Julian was due to ring her back at five, she would tell him to come down to Monk's Mead himself and find out. Mrs Grant could hardly keep him out of his own house.

Julian had never really recovered from that "fall downstairs" in London last winter. He had obviously picked up a bit of rough trade and been beaten up. It worried Barbara that he was still taking such risks, a man in his position ought to have stopped having dealings with male prostitutes long ago. He had been looking strained and drawn for months. She had suspected for some time that he was being blackmailed.

TEN

ONCE MORE UNTO the breach, dear friends, once more, Celia thought as she gave a repeat performance of evasiveness about Mary's state of mind. This time it was on the telephone, in reply to insistent questioning by Julian.

"My secretary says she seems to have developed some grievance against me. D'you know what it is?"

It was simplest, Celia had discovered, to stick to generalized psychological claptrap. "I believe it's fairly common for a woman in a nervous breakdown situation to feel threatened by her husband."

"But does she accuse me of anything in particular?"

"I'm not sure, she seems very confused."

"Barbara Seymour met with an hysterical display of hostility, she tells me."

"It's understandable. Fear of being supplanted by the 'other woman' is one of the classic symptoms."

"Poor girl, what a nonsensical idea." Julian thought for a moment. "I'd better come down, I can probably talk her out of it. Let me see. . . . Unfortunately I have a dinner date tonight with some Arabs, I'll have to keep that, but there's nothing tomorrow that I can't cancel. I'll drive down tomorrow morning and see what I can do."

Thinking it over afterwards Julian was pleased with this arrangement. Mary's illness gave him an excuse for being away from the office while the attack on the security van was taking place. When the news broke he would not have to produce expressions of surprise and horror convincing enough to deceive observant colleagues.

The Arabs and their dinner were mythical, of course. He had

171

decided to disappear again, and not be anywhere where he could be found until de Courcy's attack on the van was safely over. One never knew, something might go wrong. It had even occurred to him once or twice to wonder whether that marvellous stroke of luck in Patterson's office hadn't been too good to be true, there had been something a little odd that day about Patterson's manner. It was probably imagination, everything had been reassuringly normal since. With his money safely in the Lausanne bank he could stop hiding from de Courcy, so he had reappeared from his mythical business trip to Aberdeen and spent the afternoon in the office, without noticing anything to alarm him. It was probably a wise precaution to spend tomorrow morning allegedly in transit between his flat and Monk's Mead, and arrive there after the van had been safely hijacked. Just in case anything went wrong. . . .

Celia duly reported to Matthews on her telephone conversation with Julian and expressed the hope that he would be met by a police reception committee when he arrived at Monk's Mead.

"That depends when he gets there, Mrs Grant. Until the raid takes place, we won't have any evidence that he's committed an offence, but don't you worry. We'll have him under police observation from now on till the whole thing's over."

"Then he's turned up again, Inspector?"

"That's right, he walked into his office today at midday and we put him under observation at once. We've no idea where he's been or why, it's most puzzling."

By the evening Celia had decided that keeping people calm for long periods was about as exhausting as playing in the final of the Men's Singles at Wimbledon. Barbara's ignominious retreat had over-excited Mary, who was striding about the house talking nonsense at the top of her voice, with Celia trailing after her with a glass of water and the rejected sedative. Adam, alarmed by Mary's distraught behaviour, had become a frightened mother's boy, following Celia around and demanding constant reassurance. Tessa alone remained stationary. She was prostrate in the living room in an agony of repentance, believing that she had sent her grandmother mad by breaking the news of Peter Barton's death to her too brutally.

In addition to cooking dinner for four and providing consolation as appropriate, Celia had to console Inspector Matthews on the telephone. He rang to report dejectedly that Julian Lindsay had given him the slip and disappeared again. Duly observed by plain-clothes detectives, he had driven from his office to his flat and gone inside after parking his Rover some distance up the street in one of the few vacant spaces at the kerb. The plain-clothes men had continued their observations, but had failed till too late to observe that behind the building was a communal garden shared with several other blocks of flats, that the person emerging from the third block along the street was Lindsay, and that the car being driven away rapidly was his Rover.

"He saw we were tailing him and deliberately shook us off," said Matthews gloomily. "He knows we're on to him, he's probably warned de Courcy and told him to cancel."

"Not necessarily," Celia objected. "There could be other explanations."

"For instance?"

Celia produced a few theories off the top of her head. All were rejected as too fanciful.

"He's gone into hiding once already and reappeared," she argued. "This may be a repeat of the same pattern."

"So you say, but what's the pattern?"

"Goodness knows," said Celia. "But what do I do if he turns up here as arranged tomorrow morning?"

"Don't worry, Mrs Grant. "We'll have Monk's Mead under observation from six a.m. tomorrow. If he shows up there, we'll find some pretext for detaining him till it's all over."

By nine next morning it was very hot. Too hot for a job like this, Matthews thought as, at 9.23, the van from North London Security Services pulled out of the loading bay at Buckhurst Pressings in Chingford and embarked on the last leg of its

173

journey, through the depressing streets of north-east London. It now purported to contain all the components needed to construct a dozen of Patterson's improved guidance systems for the SS–7 missile. In fact it contained piled-up cartons of junk, with two armed policemen hiding behind them. From now on it and its load of rubbish would be at risk all the way to its destination at RGP Electronics off Hanger Lane.

The shadowing force consisted of three miscellaneous vehicles, all linked by radio telephone, with two more waiting in reserve half way along the route. There would always be one of them in front of the security van and one behind, but with plenty of room for de Courcy's attacking force to muscle its way in between them and the van.

Inspector Matthews was beside the driver in what looked like a baker's delivery truck, wondering whether or not this whole exercise was pointless. He had half expected that the attack, if any, would come as the van drove out of the yard at Buckhurst Pressings into a broad, quiet street. It would be going slowly enough to be very vulnerable, and the getaway routes were good. But nothing had happened. Probably nothing would.

The traffic through Chingford was thin. If de Courcy's hirelings were shadowing the van they were being very unobtrusive. The procession turned out of Hall's Lane into the relative security of the North Circular Road, which was double track at that point and full of fast traffic. Ahead were roundabouts and traffic lights and other potential trouble spots where a check might make an attack possible. Almost certainly, de Courcy had been warned and called the operation off, but one had to remain alert.

Palmer's Green loomed ahead, and still nothing had happened. The baker's truck with the Inspector in it took station again at the tail of the convoy, relieving a tatty-looking Ford Escort that had been on the job for the past two miles. There was a minibus between it and the security van, taking labourers to some job, just the sort of vehicle to arouse suspicion. And — yes, this was a good place for a hold-up. The traffic had narrowed to a single lane. Pipe-laying seemed to be going on in a ditch along the kerb and there was earth-moving equipment parked by the roadside.

It happened very suddenly. A dumper parked on the verge lowered its bucket in front of the security van to halt it. Men with sawn-off shotguns poured out of the minibus and surrounded the van, shouting to the driver to open up.

Matthews was surprised but not nervous, the situation was under control. The enemy plan, clearly, was to drive the van across the central reservation and away in the direction it had come from, to be unloaded at leisure in some lock-up garage rented for the purpose. But the driver and his mate had their instructions. After cutting the ignition at a hidden switch which the attackers would have trouble finding, they were to agree to open up but take plenty of time over it. Meanwhile the attackers would be rounded up by the escorting force of police, aided by those already in the van.

This is what would have happened if the dumper had not raised its bucket again and crashed it through the toughened glass of the van's windscreen. There was no need for the crew to open up. One of the attackers had climbed in through the shattered screen. Two more followed, brandishing their shotguns. Taken by surprise, the crew had not had time to reach for the hidden ignition switch. The van lurched across the central grass and into the other carriageway, where it swung about wildly in the fast traffic as the policemen and attackers on board struggled for control. A Ford Granada, cruising along serenely at seventy, hit it broadside. Matthews shut his eyes and counted as car after car added itself to the pile-up with a resounding crash. His nightmare was happening after all.

There was one consolation. All the attackers were rounded up. But it was only a partial consolation, for de Courcy was not among them.

Much as Jack de Courcy enjoyed the sound of battle with sawn-off shotguns, he had always recognized that a scene of violence on the North Circular Road was no place for a gentleman of seventy who was no longer agile. Grimshaw and

175

the others were very experienced and he had given them very detailed instructions. They understood and respected his decision to stay away, and, as it turned out, there was other work for him to do. Urgent work, resulting from a disagreeable surprise.

Three hours before the scheduled time of the hijack he was crouched over the wheel of his Jaguar and threading his way through the early morning commuter traffic making for the car parks at the Surrey railway stations. He bullied his way through a too-small overtaking gap, then made everyone brake again in a panic as he turned right without warning into the lane leading to Monk's Mead. He had enjoyed that. When he was in a really bad Low, driving scarily and putting the fear of God into people made him feel a lot better.

Thanks to that pouf Lindsay, his carefully laid plans had gone completely wrong, and he was in his worst Low for months.

It really rankled having to pay out all that money, and he had always intended to get it back. Lindsay, knowing him, would expect him to try and would take avoiding action, he would vanish abroad as soon as the fun started and make himself as difficult as possible to trace. The obvious course, therefore, was to kidnap him and make him disgorge the money *after* he had made his last business-as-usual appearance at the office and *before* the hijack took place. Lindsay would not expect that.

Or so de Courcy had thought, but he was wrong.

No one was going to take all that money off him, though. He was going to get it all back, if there was any trouble he'd start cutting Lindsay's fingers off one by one till he paid back every penny. But first, Lindsay had to be found. This was what had gone wrong.

In accordance with their agreement, Lindsay had put in an appearance at RGP Electronics yesterday afternoon. De Courcy had had him followed back to his London flat, where he had been seen to go in. But the watchers had not seen him come out again. Later that evening, when the kidnapping party arrived, there was no reply to its ring. At three in the morning, after much hesitation, de Courcy had told them to break the door down and never mind if the noise alerted the neighbours. Only then, confronted with an empty mare's nest, did de Courcy realize that he had been tricked.

Had Lindsay gone to Monk's Mead to spend his last night before leaving the country? It was possible. He would feel safe there, thinking that de Courcy would be too busy with the hijack preparations to pursue him from London. He might have treasured possessions to collect, instructions to give to his family about what to say to the police and press after he disappeared. . . . It was a long shot, but as de Courcy forced an oncoming car into the ditch, it jacked him up out of his Low for a moment and persuaded him that it was a real possibility. In any case going to Monk's Mead satisfied his thirst for action, which was a polite name for revenge. If Lindsay was not there, he could at least bully his family into telling him what they knew. Giving them a really rough time would be a pleasure.

The policeman hidden behind the thicket of Garland roses spoke softly into his walkie-talkie to his colleague on the far side of the house, beyond the lily pool. "Someone's just driven into the forecourt in a Jag. Elderly gent."

"Lindsay, is it?"

"Wait, he's getting out. . . . No, definitely not. Quite a lot older. . . . He's rung the bell. . . . Mrs Grant's come to the door and they're talking in the doorway. . . . He's gone into the house."

"Probably the family doctor come to see Lady Lindsay."

"Bit early for that, isn't it?"

"Not if she was taken bad in the night."

"Good morning, madam," said de Courcy, stepping into the hall. "Inspector Williams, Metropolitan Police, I'd like a word with Sir Julian Lindsay."

Celia stared at him in amazement. He had flashed a card with a photograph on it at her, but too fast for her to see what it was. Among the many reasons why he could not be Inspector

177

Williams, Metropolitan Police, the one uppermost in her mind was that he was far too old. He reminded her of a television actor who had gone on playing a kindly policeman till well on in his seventies, what was the name of that series? Oh yes, *Dixon of Dock Green.*

Meanwhile de Courcy was taking stock of Celia. Tiny. Fragile and excitingly helpless looking. Some kind of lady housekeeper, no doubt, unlikely to give much trouble. But was Lindsay in the house? Who else was? Where was Lady Lindsay? He had rushed to Monk's Mead without a clear plan, only an immense anger.

Celia simpered up at him with wide, innocent eyes. He had a gun-shaped bulge under his jacket. This ludicrous and bewildering development would have to be taken seriously. Gathering her wits she said: "Perhaps you'd tell me what you want to see Sir Julian about."

"I'd prefer to state my business to him personally," said de Courcy. "He came down from London last night, I understand."

On thinking carefully, Celia decided not to disillusion him; and further, that alarm signals from one of the bedroom windows would be seen by the watching police. "He arrived very late last night, and he's not down yet. I'll just run up and knock on his door and tell him you're here."

"I'll come upstairs with you, madam, if I may," said de Courcy. If he could get her and Lindsay together in one room, the beginnings of a strategy might emerge.

"Very well, Inspector, I'll be with you in a moment." Changing her tactics, she dodged past him towards the front door.

He followed and grabbed her fiercely by the arm. "Where are you going, madam?"

Celia gave a loud wail, inspired by genuine terror as well as a desire to summon the waiting police.

"Stop that noise, madam, at once."

"Let go of my arm, you're hurting me," she shrieked, even louder.

178

De Courcy resisted the temptation to knock her down and kick her. An outcry at this stage would rouse the household, perhaps bring Lindsay to the head of the stairs with a shotgun. He relaxed his grip.

"Really, Inspector," said Celia, massaging her arm and eyeing him like a hurt kitten. "You men don't know your strength." Evidently her shriek had not been loud enough to bring the police to her aid, but she had remembered two blessed facts; her keys were in her pocket, and she had left the back door open when she let the cat out for its morning walk.

"I am investigating a criminal matter," said de Courcy severely, "and I wish to interview Sir Julian Lindsay. Stop playing about and take me to him at once."

"Of course, when I've reset the burglar alarm. I switched it off to let you in."

"That's quite unnecessary in the day time," he snapped.

"Oh, but Lady Lindsay insists. A man was murdered in the drive and she's been terrified ever since."

She slipped the key into the control box by the front door and turned it. The twenty-second warning tone started. She smiled charmingly at him as they waited for it to stop and set the alarm.

He panicked. There was something odd about the smile. This was some kind of trap. "Turn that thing off at once and come upstairs with me."

"Oh, I seem to have dropped the key, how stupid of me. Can you see it anywhere?"

Before he could start looking, a fearful clamour broke out; a shrill whistle inside the house and a clanging bell on the wall outside. The open back door had set off the alarm.

De Courcy wrenched open the front door to make for the Jaguar and get clear. The policeman hiding in the forecourt ran forward towards the house. De Courcy fired at him twice, as he took cover behind the Jaguar. De Courcy ran back into the house, slammed the front door shut, threw the bolt and began dragging Celia towards the stairs. And three cruising police cars switched on their sirens on receiving a radio message that the burglar alarm at Monk's Mead had gone off.

Julian Lindsay sat in the Rover in Richmond Park, listening to Radio London for news of the hold-up. As soon as he heard that it was safely over he would drive on to Monk's Mead and break the glad news to Mary that they were going on holiday to Austria and that he had tickets for the opera in Salzburg. She would probably raise objections connected with that wretched garden, and his own and Barbara's enquiries through Mrs Grant (who must be got rid of promptly, in case she interfered) suggested that Mary was in a slightly more mutinous mood than usual. But if he made her feel guilty enough about spoiling the lovely surprise treat he had prepared for her, she would do what she was told in the end.

He had already rung Patterson to say that his wife's illness had taken an alarming turn, that her doctor advised complete rest and change, and that he would have to take a few days off while he settled her into a psychiatric clinic. No need to say yet that he would be taking her abroad.

It was almost eleven. The traffic news before the bulletin included a warning of a multiple pile-up on the North Circular Road, which was causing a long tail-back. Wondering idly whether it had interfered with de Courcy's arrangements, he listened to the bulletin. No news yet. He would drive out of London, listen to the next bulletin at twelve, and arrive at Monk's Mead in time for lunch.

Radio London was dispensing crude and raucous music, but he left it open. As he circled the Esher by-pass, it stopped abruptly for a news flash. The trouble on the North Circular Road was caused by an attempted hold-up which had gone wrong. The police, apparently acting on a tip-off, had foiled an attempt to steal secret military equipment from a van belonging to a security company. All the attackers had been arrested.

Feeling sick and giddy, Lindsay pulled in to the kerb, with renewed pop music blaring from the car radio. He must go abroad at once. No. The police had known all along, had earmarked him as the dupe who would lead de Courcy into the trap. The channel ferries and the airports would be watched, he would be arrested the moment he produced his passport.

His palms were clammy. He seemed to have lost the ability to analyse a tricky situation calmly and decide what course of action would produce the least disastrous result. It took him almost half an hour of utter mental confusion to decide that the only person he could turn to for shelter and help was Barbara Seymour.

Barbara Seymour was in a panic. She had spent the morning in London, giving evidence to yet another Select Committee of the House of Commons. At Waterloo Station on the way home she had bought an early edition of the evening paper containing a front-page story about an attempted hold-up involving a van full of secret guided missile equipment manufactured by RGP Electronics, the firm Julian worked for. He was mentioned in the story as a director of the firm. His absence from his office and London flat, and the fact that the telephone receiver seemed to be off at his "luxurious" country home in Surrey, were touched on in the guarded language used when newspapers know something, but are playing safe with the law.

In the train she reviewed all the little danger signals of the past few months, the things that had made her suspect that he was in some kind of trouble, probably blackmail. It looked from the hints in the paper as if he was in very hot water indeed, in which case all sorts of skeletons might come tumbling out of their cupboards, including some which would be very inconvenient from her own point of view. It was terrifying, she had to know, she would ask him. He would be at Monk's Mead looking after Mary, he had phoned her last night to say so. She collected her car at Guildford Station to drive straight there, and switched on her car radio in time to catch a news item about a siege at the country home of Sir Julian Lindsay, a director of RGP Electronics, who, etcetera etcetera. . . .

It seemed a nightmare, but it was true. As she approached Monk's Mead a policeman waved her on down the lane. The garden must have been cleared of visitors, the only vehicles in the car park were the sort that converge on the scene of a long-drawn-out house siege, cars belonging to the police and television crews, and a mobile canteen supplying cups of tea. Beyond the Wild Garden someone was talking into a loud hailer.

She drove on down the lane as if the devil was behind her, to distance herself from a disgrace which could not, must not, have anything to do with her. Julian must be desperate if he was holed up in the house with a shotgun, resisting arrest. It was horrifying, the siege would end, Julian would shoot himself or surrender, there would be enormous publicity. Wrongdoing in high places with a homosexual background delighted the press, the whole story of 1941 would come out, her name would be dragged through the mud with his. The newshounds would take no time at all to unearth the fact that Sir Julian Lindsay was the real 'Kit' of the Mortlock love-poems, and that Miss Barbara Seymour, CBE, the well-known educationalist and authority on social questions, had invented a love affair between herself and Anthony Mortlock to cover up for him. She would be a laughing stock, her public life would be over, and as she had never bothered to have much of a private life, the future would be very bleak indeed.

She was damned if she was going to let that happen. A mile down the lane she parked by the roadside to think. A gut reaction of fear had made her pass by beleaguered Monk's Mead on the other side like the Pharisee, but was there nothing she could do to avert the threatened disaster? Yes, there was. She would create a diversion, give Julian a chance to slip out through the police cordon, and — yes, smuggle him abroad. Then there would be no trial, no evidence given on oath that could not be denied. If there was no trial, whatever mud the press chose to fling at her could be dismissed as slander and speculation.

Her scarf, her handkerchief, an old sweater she found in the boot, one after another she stuffed them down the neck of the fuel tank and pulled them out again. Then she set off on foot to the far side of the Wild Garden, by a route through fields that

182

the police were unlikely to know.

De Courcy saw it before the police did. Behind them a wall of fire was creeping steadily forward from tree to tree. The Wild Garden was like tinder at the end of a dry summer and the wind was brisk. The policemen covering the house from across the lawn came out from behind the tree trunks and ran about, half hidden in the smoke.

The fire was running about too, along the pergola and the yew hedge, through the bank of azaleas, up towards the house. Blessedly, the smoke was getting thicker and blacker. Soon there would be enough of it to cover his escape. As it billowed around he waited for a thick patch, then slipped out into the yard with the dustbins and through a smouldering hedge into a field. Out in the lane he dodged round a screaming fire engine on its way to the rescue, and made for the main road. Although he had used the gun there were still three rounds in it. He could hold up a car and be miles away before the police realized he was no longer in the house. There were two women upstairs in a bedroom tied to chairs, but it served them right.

ELEVEN

THE FIREMEN MANAGED to save the house, but the garden was a charred wreck, impossible to restore to anything like its original state. Adam Lindsay was overjoyed. It had been a millstone round his neck. It had prevented him from following a career, it had wrecked his marriage. It had grown out of shape till it was a grotesque parody of Gertrude Jekyll's intentions, no longer worth preserving as a piece of gardening history. And now it was gone for ever.

He managed somehow to keep his feelings to himself. For his mother's sake there had to be a decent period of mourning for the deceased garden, but his head was full of plans. He would move nearer London and enrol as a mature student at an art school. He would persuade his wife back, the garden was the only thing that had come between them. Together they would make a home for Tessa.

I am prostrate with grief, Mary Lindsay told herself. Of course I am, not to be would be indecent and would shock Mother very much. But if I am as prostrate as all that, why do I have to force myself not to giggle when I think of the charred stumps where that hellish pergola used to be, with the wisteria on it that took a week of backache to prune? I must control myself and not giggle. I must concentrate on the real question, which is who the hell am I? I used to be a woman who looked after a tyrannical mother and an equally tyrannical garden and put up with an even more tyrannical husband, but who am I now? How the hell do I solve my problem of identity?

I shall sell Monk's Mead, that house is far too big. I shall move into a cottage and have a garden full of the things I like instead of being hedged about with bossy old Gertrude's rules and regulations. I couldn't grow this because she said it was in bad taste, and I couldn't grow that because it wasn't in cultivation till after she died, and if I did anything she anathematized somebody would produce a copy of Gertrude's Holy Writ and rub my nose in it, as if I was a puppy being house-trained. I think I shall go in for carpet bedding just to show her. Stiff rows of geraniums in the colours she hated, and nasty little pink begonias with chocolate brown leaves, planted in circles round hideous spotty abutilons, and the stuff that looks like green and crimson vomit, what is it called? Oh yes, Love-Lies-Bleeding, that would make the fat old thing spin like a top in her grave.

Does Adam mind about the garden? He's been very secretive lately. Who the hell was his father, I shall make Barbara tell me. He won't mind when I divorce Julian, he's always hated him.

Celia's first task after the Monk's Mead debacle was to stimulate the thought processes of the police. It had not occurred to Matthews that if he wanted to locate and arrest Julian Lindsay he should arrange at once to eavesdrop on Barbara Seymour's telephone, because it was a safe bet that he would ring Barbara and tell her where he was, so that she could come to his help. Matthews was doubtful at first, but as usual she was right and Lindsay was arrested at the motorway service centre where he had arranged to meet Barbara.

Also at her suggestion, Matthews persuaded the press not to publish for the present the fact that Lindsay was safely under arrest. During what the papers described as her Ordeal, she had gathered from de Courcy that Lindsay had extorted a lot of money from him, and that his main aim in life was to find Lindsay and get it back. She had taken to visiting Barbara Seymour almost daily, on the pretext of putting their heads together about Mary Lindsay's future and the death-throes of the Monk's Mead Trust. What Barbara did not know was that when Celia left her she always drove away looking as furtive as possible to a seedy bungalow in Godalming into which, with ostentatious precautions against being observed, she carried covered dishes of food.

185

Fortunately it had occurred to de Courcy almost at once that if he wanted to find Lindsay, his confidante Barbara Seymour was the person to watch. After only three repeats of Celia's performance the penny dropped and de Courcy followed her to Godalming. Raring to settle accounts with Lindsay, he burst into the suspect bungalow and was warmly received by the patient police constables whom Celia had been feeding.

Matthews had assumed that the Wild Garden at Monk's Mead had been set on fire by some accomplice of de Courcy's, anxious to help him escape. Celia did not think it necessary to point out his error. Barbara would suffer enough from the publicity when the case came to court.

When it did, her sufferings were considerable. For almost a week even the combined forces of a royal baby, a hijacked airliner with British passengers on board, and a row in parliament about the alleged wickedness of the police, were not sufficient to drive off the front pages the juicy details of Julian Lindsay's misbehaviour and her part in it.

JOHN SHERWOOD is a very well-known British mystery writer whose books include *A Botanist at Bay, Green Trigger Fingers, Death at The BBC, The Disappearance Of Dr. Bruderstein,* and others. He lives in Kent, in the south of England.